As if it wasn't bad enough to have a mad doctor injecting me with hallucinogenic drugs, they kept bashing me in the head...

I'd been playing for time, of course. The look on the doctor's face told me that he'd known it all along. "We act like we control our lives, but we don't."

"With germ warfare?"

"Nothing so primitive. My 'treatment' is a designed drug that will cure a terrible condition which has gone on for far too long. People are suffering and ethics will do nothing to help them. Medical science stopped polio and gave the treatment to every child in your country, as if it were the law. But it took a dying president and a March of Dimes to do it. Nobody cares to cure cycle cell anemia in Negroes yet, or autism, or Parkinson's disease. But now they will. Now, when the threat becomes big enough. In order to save all those who suffer, I'm making the threat big enough to demand notice."

I realized that any further arguments would only make things worse. I began imagining that this was possibly the end. The thought stiffened every muscle in my body.

The Chinese Guy came into view. He whispered something to the mad doctor. Something containing the words, "boss" and "problem."

Dr. Z rested a hand gently on the other man's forearm. Rosita stepped between them. The doctor shook his head reluctantly. "All right. You handle it, and I'll get things together."

Rosita remained silent, but her eyes searched back at me.

The Gun Guy spun his weapon in his huge hand and brought the butt end down hard on my crown. Too late, I called out, "Cliché," as my entire head and everything else went black, just like my eyes.

In October 1959, a young, hard-luck PI is lost in America, determined to untangle a series of grisly murders spreading like a disease from the set of *The Alamo*. Fighting for his life—from a dry desert storm, to a mind-bending fog in San Francisco, and a snow-blinding mountain top outside Hollywood—LA PI Stan Wade gropes his way through drug-induced false trails, trying to outwit an aggressive, obsessive mass murderer.

KUDOS for Stormfall

"A trip back to 1959 that starts on the shooting location of The Alamo almost becomes the last stand of Stan Wade, Hollywood PI. Along the way, there's much fast-paced, lighthearted action, numerous surprise cameos, and enough celebrity name dropping to make Louella and Hedda jealous." ~ Terence Faherty, Shamus award winner and author of the Scott Elliott series

"As always, Hegenberger does a great job of vividly recreating a time and place, adding plenty of period details without overwhelming his breakneck-paced plot. The Stan Wade series is one of the most purely entertaining around, and STORMFALL is another great one." ~ James Reasoner, award-winning author of Texas Wind and over 150 other fine novels

Praise for other Stan Wade, LA PI novels

"In SUPERFALL John Hegenberger takes us on an irresistible, hard-boiled walk down memory lane, with P.I. Stan Wade as the perfect tour guide. From George Reeves to Lloyd Bridges to Ross Macdonald, this is a historical tour-de-force." ~ Robert J. Randisi, President of the Private Eye Writers of America

STORMFALL

A Stan Wade, LA PI Novel

John Hegenberger

A Black Opal Books Publication

DEDICATION

For Johnny, my Number One Son

"One question that everyone wanted to know was, just exactly where in Bracketville was LaJean going to be living? The rumourmongers, of course, came up with possible answers, and they all pointed to John Wayne and his reputation as a ladies' man." ~ Michael Munn, *The Hollywood Murder Case Book*

"But I have never had too high a regard for what is generally called "reality. Reality, to me, is not so much something that you perceive, but something you make." ~ Philip K. Dick, 1972

Let's all remember that what follows is a work of "faction" based entirely on the author's dreams, recollections, and speculations. None of the names have been changed to protect anyone. All of the events *almost* occurred exactly as reported.

PROLOGUE

October, 1959:

Thunder rumbled outside the rented apartment as Chet thought that he sure could use a wet sloppy kiss. He giggled the way he always did when he was high. He knew that the dope had made him slow and clumsy, but he didn't care. The price had been right and he was feeling the singing in his veins and head.

Jean floated in. She bent and scooped up her copy of the script from the coffee table where his feet were propped in front of the snow-filled TV set.

He made a pass at grabbing her arm, but missed. "Hey, where you going, baby? It's after three in the goddamn morning?"

"I told you. I'm leaving, Chet. You slobs are never going to amount to anything. Hank and Doug are happy to sleep together and you—you drink and take too many pills."

"Nahhh…" was all he could say. "I—I love you, sugerbabe, you know that." The old excitement was starting to rise. It happened whenever he saw her. "Let's do it here. On the couch."

Jean tossed her blonde hair and screwed up her face. "I told you, Chet. I'm leaving."

And she took her sweet butt into the bedroom, emerging seconds later with a suitcase and armload of coat-hangered clothes.

His mouth felt dry as old newspaper. He struggled to his feet. "You—you can't do that."

"I'm doing it. Wayne has a room for me closer to the set. He's expanding my part, giving me more lines. You guys are weighing me down." She dropped her luggage and dresses beside the apartment's front door and went back into the bedroom for another load.

Chet felt the rage bubbling up. His hands flexed as his gaze wobbled across the room to the sharp prop they had given him for his role in the picture. The blade was only five inches long, shaped like a Bowie knife. It would go all the way into the cheating bitch's heart.

Someone said, "Kill her," or maybe it was just another roll of thunder. Chet saw that he was alone with only the sound of the TV's hissing static.

His hand was drawn to the knife. He studied an eye in its reflective surface. *No*, he thought, *no I didn't, but...How has it gotten into my hand? And why am I carrying it toward...toward the bedroom?*

She acted startled to see him so close. *Acted.*

His palm itched. He rotated the handle and drove the blade all the way into her chest.

Her mouth and eyes widened, like tulips. She flailed for a second and seemed to turn into a fawn in his arms. *Soft brown eyes. Sweet small tongue.*

Then she folded and a low moan slid out of her. She said that she loved him, and his hand grew wet and warm and red. The doctor's finest drugs sang to him.

"I love you too, sugarbabe. Gimme a kiss."

Outside, the rain beat down in sheets on the roof. *Or is that someone pounding on the door?*

PART I
DUSTSTORM

CHAPTER 1

I had no way of knowing then, but the next week of my life would be filled with duststorms, snowstorms, and brainstorms. How? Easy. It began in the arid, windswept valleys of Texas and ended on top of Mount Baldy, and in between, I was drugged to the gills by an intellectual who hated the way our country treated "his people."

On a Tuesday in mid-October 1959, I was on page 71 of the digest version of *Woman in the Dark*, where "Conroy fell away from the fist rigidly, with unbent knees," when my phone rang. I hadn't read a lot of Hammett, but this tale didn't impress me as much as the one earlier that afternoon—a Continental Op story called, *Slippery Fingers*.

I flexed my own fingers, put the paperback on the edge of my desk, and answered the phone, feeling hard-boiled due to my choice of reading material. "Stan Wade, Private Investigations. We never blink."

The female voice on the end of the line commanded sweetly, "Hold for Mr. Ford." Then in a more submissive tone, I heard, "He's on the phone, sir."

"Is this Wade?"

I acknowledged my last name, and the gruff guy went on. "I need you here now. Drop what you're damn-well doin' and get to the airport out in Anaheim. There'll be a flight waiting for you on the executive runway to-morrow morning at seven o'clock."

The paperback tilted, about to flop on the floor. "Ex-cuse me—A flight? To where?"

The book dropped into the wastebasket on top of the remains of a slice of raspberry pie—a la mode.

"San Antonio. I'll have a man meet you there with a car and a check for eight hundred dollars. That ought to cover your first week."

I was fighting the first signs of a cold and sore throat, so I popped another Smith Brother's cough drop in my mouth and talked around it. "Is this really John Ford, the director?"

The receiver rattled in my ear. "Hell, yes, I'm Ford. You returned my call and now I'm calling you back."

I tasted cherry on the back of my tongue and glanced through the open door as a waiter dashed by carrying a tray of heavenly-smelling sirloins. "I remember now. Sorry, I'm just finishing up with slippery case involving a woman…in the dark."

"What's wrong with you, boy? Say, do you want this job or not? Disney said you were a top investigator, but you sound out of focus to me."

I stifled a sneeze from the cold or the subtle scent of our LA smog. "Okay, take it easy." The mention of Walt finally sold me. I'd worked for the elder cartoonist on several discreet cases and if Ford knew even a smidgen about them, it meant this phone call was the real thing. "What am I expected to do for your eight hundred?"

"Christ on a stick, kid. You're supposed to show up and solve a murder." The line slammed shut with the sound of a cheap cap gun.

I flexed a finger at the receiver and immediately felt stupid for doing it.

The soggy novel lay in the trash, and I wondered if Conroy ever got up.

☙❧

The clock in the hall above the restaurant's time cards said it was half-past four. I'd need at least an hour to drive across town via Santa Monica Boulevard in rush-hour traffic to my boat in del Rey and pack a bag. My swivel chair creaked and almost tipped over as I got up. Damn, those steaks smelled good.

I opened a desk drawer and shrugged into my .38 shoulder holster. I slipped a worn sport jacket over the holster and gun and remembered that I had a change of clothes hanging in Suzi's closet. Going there, instead of the *Cervantes II*, would cut twenty minutes from the drive in the morning, since the 101 ran all the way from North Hollywood down to Orange County. Still, considering the morning traffic, it might be quicker if I just drove straight to San Antonio.

When I locked up my tiny office and ducked out the rear of the Brown Derby, I stopped to grab a steak sandwich and consider Ford's word "murder." The wide-open spaces of Texas would be a welcome change from all the complex highway logistics of LA.

೨೦೮೦

Suzi handed me a light-blue Oxford with a button-down collar. "He wants you to go to Texas?" I didn't remember seeing this shirt before. She was always buying me clothes, as if somehow it would make a better man of me. Fat chance.

"Eight-hundred a week," I reminded her. "That's better than our usual fifty per day."

We were both in the PI business. Only she was planning on raising her rates—for good reason. Suzi Sunset had a full-service agency with offices in the Taft building. I had a battered desk at the back of a restaurant where I gently enforced deadbeats who didn't pay their bar bills.

The love of my life and soon to be wife stepped back, tilting her honey-colored head to one side, inspecting me. "I've said it before, Standy, you should raise your rates. I told Jerry Lewis last night after his *Jazz Singer* show at NBC that I charged a hundred a day plus expenses for investigative work. He didn't bat an eye." She handed me a couple of pairs of socks and a small stack of handkerchiefs. I made certain that there were no frilly edges.

"That's probably because you batted those baby blues at him. Which, I can't do." I stuffed underwear into my suitcase and clicked the latches shut. "And wouldn't if I could."

Her face seemed to glow slightly. "And that's why I love and will miss you. Why have you been gone so much lately?" She let those same wild blue-yonders skewer me.

That was all it took. Within minutes, we were enjoying a frisky evening's skewering.

Later, we hugged long and sincerely—and drifted off together. I never did answer her question.

☙❧

There was a soft buttery glow in the east now. The car's radio beat out the latest rock-and-roll tunes on

KFWB-98, and the sun would soon beat down on the shimmering concrete roadway. I hated heavy traffic, but this morning's didn't seem too bad.

I drove south on the Hollywood freeway around a Greyhound Bus and then got stuck behind a ratty pick-up full of Mexican day laborers. Despite the forty-mile-an-hour speed of several passing delivery trucks, the Latinos stood shoulder to shoulder in the back of their banged-up Dodge, chatting, laughing, and lighting cigarettes off each other's butts. I gave them a two-finger salute as I swung past, but they didn't seem to notice. They occupied a place in my world, but at the same time were in their own private version of it. *Vaya con Dios, amigos.*

I concentrated on steering through the interchange with Route 66 past the city proper. After navigating a knot of semi-stalled vehicles, I relaxed and began to reflect on what I knew of the crusty John Ford.

He was an ex-military man with a thirty-year career of directing motion pictures, thus accustomed to having his orders carried out without question. Working for Ford would be tricky, especially if I expected to handle the case my way, which is to say unhindered by his authority. I liked to follow each lead or hunch wherever it took me without "direction."

Once things started happening, there wasn't a lot of time to report every detail back to the client. I'd been cursed or blessed with a series of investigations lately that kept getting deeper and a bit out of hand. But I'd come through them all with some success, if not a lot of cold cash. October, 1959 would be…let's see…the fifth full year of operating the agency on my own.

A full year, too, with more things going wrong than a season of *I Love Lucy*. Since spring, I'd dealt with dead astronauts, sunken treasure, and Soviet spies. I'd flown a hover platform over Germany, run around Vegas with a supposedly dead TV star, and killed a woman intentionally. Now, I was "gone to Texas" to look into a murder that involved John Wayne and his new movie, *The Alamo*.

ഇ⊃ഌ

I parked in the wide, flat lot outside the flat, concrete Orange County Airport and began walking in the warm sunlight toward the tiny terminal. Not all places in the LA basin were exciting and colorful for the tourists. For a second, I saw double—twin images aligned side-by-side like a movie special effect. Only it wasn't anything special. It was something the docs had warned me about, after I'd been slugged in the head one time too many.

I'd need to take it easy, they said. Maybe consider a new line of work, since my life as a detective had caused me to get knocked out more times than a heavyweight fighter. Pretty soon, I'd have to start wearing a hard hat.

Occasionally, for no good reason, the world would go out of focus or slide to the right, and I'd hear a sharp ringing for a few seconds. I knew I should try and take it easy, relax for a few weeks on a quiet vacation, instead of taking on any new sleuthing clients. But I couldn't resist a good case when it came my way. Besides, I needed the dough for my upcoming wedding. So, like a dutiful mailman, I pressed on, no matter the climate, and kept my self-appointed rounds, this time with prepaid airfare.

The plane was little more than a puddle-jumper. It didn't have to be big, just fast enough to make the trip past Phoenix and El Paso to San Antonio. Most of the other passengers were employed in some capacity with the movie. I was delighted to find that my old acquaintance, Joe Canutt, was aboard.

I knew Joe and his father from my brief spell as an apprentice stuntman in the early '50s. He was already enjoying a pre-flight scotch when I plunked down in the seat beside him.

Canutt smiled when he saw me and indicated his plastic cup of amber liquid. "Keeps me sane."

I never touched the stuff anymore and ordered a Pepsi. "Hey, Joe. You running a dangerous gag for Wayne's pic?"

"Not as dangerous as your job, Stan. I heard you almost fell off the Capitol Records Tower a month ago."

Joe knew I was a licensed snoop and kind of envied me for it. Anything near danger and death interested him. "Just another day of routine maintenance work." The stewardess brought my soda pop and I let the bubbles tickle my nose.

He half-turned in his seat. "Hey, how about that George Reeves dying, huh? I worked with him on a Disney western couple of years back. Even then, he'd packed on a lot of weight for a superman. Too bad he ate his gun, huh?"

"Too damn bad," I agreed as I buckled in.

After a bouncing roll out to the runway, our plane lunged up and accelerated away into the eastern sky. I knew that Reeves was still down there below us somewhere, alive and kicking, but I couldn't tell Canutt or anyone else the true story.

Joe asked how I was involved with the Alamo movie, and I told him I wouldn't know for sure until I met with John Ford.

Canutt gave me a nodding "yeah, yeah" and took a pack of Old Gold's from his shirt pocket and shook one out at me. "Smoke?"

"No thanks. I don't anymore."

He shrugged, put them away, and caught an attendant's eye, signaling for a refill of his drink. "Tread easy around Pappy, huh? And don't try any funny stuff with Wayne, either." He chuckled and shook his well-tanned head. "I once caught holy hell from Duke for not being man enough during a fight scene. He damn near knocked my block off with those big fists of his." He rubbed his jaw as if he'd just been slugged.

Joe was a good foot taller than I was, with wide shoulders and somewhat bowed legs inside his worn cowboy boots. He knew plenty about taking a punch and rolling down a hill from a galloping horse, but this was the first time I'd seen him with a worry line etched between his eyes.

I drained my cup of Pepsi and sucked on a piece of ice. "Okay, pard. I'll be sure and ack tough aron' bof Ford an Wayne." I learned a long time ago that I'd get further with most Hollywood types by suppressing my boyish charm. Acting hard-boiled was a cliché, but movie people expected it from a private eye. Cops, however, hated it, but knowing the correct stance to take with people often was half of my profession. Something like method acting.

They said you couldn't smell vodka on someone's breath, but I had found that not to be the case with scotch, and soon Joe was malevolently fragrant. He continued to drink and eventually dozed through most of the trip.

I noticed a complimentary copy of *Time Magazine*, but avoided it with disgust when I saw that the cover story was about "The Corpse in the Living Room." It featured Peter Gunn, Stuart Bailey, Philip Marlowe, and Richard Diamond in an article about the private lives of all the slick new TV private eyes. I almost gagged. That kind of publicity gave the public the wrong impression. Most of professional PI work involved mundane skip tracing and process serving, although my last year *had* been uniquely adventurous. Maybe someday someone would write about my "adventures." If all else failed, I could always write it out longhand myself in my old age. Hmmm.

CHAPTER 2

The plane's engines hummed.

With little else to occupy my attention, I slipped into a light sleep beside Joe's snoring corpse. We refueled in El Paso and I got a chance to call back to Suzi.

Her voice sounded concerned and tiny on the long-distance line. "Lex has started drinking again."

"Well, after all, she's her own woman. And her fiancée does own a bar." The sun was burning high in the pale sky and I wished I'd brought my shades. "Miss you already."

"Me too, Standy. I might have a new client when you get back."

"Oh? Who?"

She laughed slightly in her throat, the way I like. "Tell you when you get back."

"Suzi Sunset, Woman of Mystery."

She laughed again and we rang off. I missed her already.

The plane set down in San Antonio around one o'clock, their time. The sun now hung high in the western sky, hot and orange. I tasted Texas dust in my mouth for the first time.

The shoulder holster began chaffing my left underarm. I considered sloughing it off the first chance I got and carrying the .38 in my jacket pocket. I could put my wallet and keys in the other side to make my sport coat hang more balanced. I didn't much like carrying the thing and actually felt less rather than more powerful, but it had saved my life more than once and, in my line of work, once is enough to make it your friend.

Out beside the passenger pick-up area, I was re-stuffing the leather assembly into my battered suitcase, when Joe pulled up in a long, black Oldsmobile. He gave me a honk and a shout to get in.

Canutt seemed sober enough, so I figured, "why not?" We swung out of the terminal traffic and headed south of the city. Minutes later, Joe grinned at me. "Here we go."

I opened the car door and found myself surrounded by a crowd of denim jackets, American flags and fancy checkered shirts with fancier neckerchiefs. A tight group of blanketed plains Indians passed in full war paint, followed by a girl in pigtails, twirling and jumping a lasso.

For a second, I thought I was dreaming in broad daylight.

"Sorry," Joe grinned, exiting the limo. "I've got to do a few publicity stunts here to promote the movie, before going on to set at Brackettville. Shouldn't take long. Enjoy yourself."

I'd never been to a true rodeo before, with calf roping and steer throwing. It was part carnival, state fair, sideshow, and horse race—all dominated by a jury-rigged grandstand and poorly painted clowns. Color-filled circus acts sprang up within the crowd as I walked along.

A fierce, ugly Negro in what looked like a matador's outfit blew out mouthfuls of fire. A young couple dressed as gunslingers juggled silver six-guns back and forth. An overland stage rattled past us, followed by a dust cloud and a passel of savages. Then some trick rider stood up in the saddle of his galloping horse and fired, chasing after them.

I sneezed and watched the dust settle. Part of me wished I could experience it all like a kid again with awe and wonder and a little joy. But the majority of folks here appeared hollow and desperate with a hunger behind their eyes, perhaps trying to live out a dream or make a fast buck. Many of the contestants limped or groaned when they stood erect. They moved slowly out of caution of the pain in their lower back.

One wrangler stuttered so bad that he spoke mostly with gestures like a silent comedian. I mentioned it to Joe who said the guy'd been knocked off his horse onto his head once too often. The doctors said his brain had swollen temporarily, causing a lack of oxygen. I rubbed the back of my neck at the hairline and quietly muttered, "Peter Piper picked a peck of pickled peppers," just to be sure.

The air circulated the smells of horse shit, gun smoke, and grilled beef.

I hadn't planned on getting suited up for the old west, but the opportunity issuing from all the booths and stalls of cowboy outfits and western clothing was too damn tempting. Recollections of the dude-ranch days of my teens came back as I stepped into pre-worn work jeans and boots with inch-high heels. The shirt I chose had button-down pockets and my soft brown vest sported leatherette roses. All I needed now were chaps and a lariat.

A burly cowpoke, who turned out to be Joe Canutt, now in full Western dress, approached. I watched in fascination as he sprinkled, licked, and actually rolled a cigarette. I think my mouth hung open a little. He smiled and removed his wide-brimmed soft hat, shoving it onto my head. Without hesitation, I pulled the lanyard tight under my chin. He nodded and lit a match on the back of his jeans. "You can stash your suitcase and street clothes in the trunk of the Olds. Here's the keys."

I decided it would be best if I left my .38 there, too. When I came back, I took a bowlegged stance, which made him laugh. "There. Now you look like a cowpoke."

"Hopalong Cassiday?"

"More like Dick Foran."

I grunted in disgust. "You must be one of the older fellows."

Not being used to wearing a wide-brimmed cow-hat, I managed to knock it into a low-hanging string of pennant flags, momentarily blinded myself. When I tilted the brim back into place, I saw an Indian chief in full thunderbird dress walking down on me, a feathered spear in one hand and a violin and bow in the other. I let him pass, offering a single word to cover my chagrin: "Ugh!" He eyed me mid-step, spat a gob of tobacco juice near my feet, and glided regally on.

A few minutes later in front of the crowd filling the grand stand, Roy Rogers pretended to have a fake shootout with Gene Autry. I was impressed to see them together, having heard, when I worked stunts back at the Republic Studios in my youth, that they hated each other. Professional jealousy, I guess. Following this silly standoff, they warbled a couple of songs in a mellow, nasally twang.

Then, just before the appearance of Bob Hope, a steer the size of a buffalo got loose in the arena. Joe jumped down, hooting and waving at the animal, and a young boy in jeans and plain white T-shirt got excited and leaned a little too far over the railing. I watched him tumble in and saw the bull do an end-run around Joe, heading for the kid. I got up on the rail, shouting, and jumped down into the soft, tan dirt. The kid was frozen in Keds by the approach of what had to be a ton of angry livestock.

I came alive, myself and grabbed the scruff of the boy's shirt, hauling him up the side of the railing to the out-stretched arms of what had to be his father. Joe wrestled the steer, getting it to veer off to the other side of the arena. The crowd thought this was a grand show, cheering and hooting for more action.

Sweat rolled down my face and adrenaline flowed into my heart and other muscles. Canutt hefted me up the railing, pushing too hard. My head hit the top of the rail smack between the eyes as I clambered over. It didn't knock me out, but it made the world seem to spin backward. People pulled me to my feet. Someone gave me a plastic bag full of ice for my forehead. It might have been Dale Evans.

I stood there dripping and weaving a little. The mother and father of the boy I'd saved from being trampled were embarrassingly appreciative that we'd saved Junior. I had a blurred image of Mr. and Mrs. Bush, relieved and thankful. Struggling to see straight, I caught my breath and repositioned the ice pack. "Shucks, ma'am, it was nothing a'tall. Glad the lad is okay."

The burr-headed kid was standing off in a small

crowd of his three younger brothers, all wearing white T-shirts and jeans. He seemed more dazed than I felt, and I wondered if it was from shock or if he always looked that way.

Georgie's folks offered to buy me the best bar-b-que dinner in Texas, but I just wanted to go sit down some-where.

That's when a dark blue Ranchero car-truck pulled up and I got my first face-to-face with Pappy Ford.

⁊⁊⁊

"Tell me again how you happened to pick me for this assignment."

Ford looked eighty, probably was sixty, with a wisp of hair over each ear. His glasses were thick enough to ignite ants. His lips reminded me to two strips of liver. His face was like melted wax with blemishes. One eye fixed me and the over was covered by black leather.

"Old Irish saying: 'Do good by stealth and blush to find it known.'" Drawing match flame into the bowl of his pipe, the famed film director went on. "I did some checking up on you. When I got an earful about your past from Walt and other industry sources, you struck me as a noble fool."

We were in the back seat of the modified and en-closed Ranchero station-wagon thing, driving west past barren land and low scrub. The vehicle was a miniature house/trailer, big enough that I could sit inside and still wear my cowboy hat.

Ford sat next to me, letting a bundle of bound papers slip from his lap to the vehicle's floor, like trash. Paunchy, he wore tan slacks a dark blue windbreaker jacket half zipped over a rumpled white shift with a dirty collar. I'd heard that they'd started giving jackets out to everyone in a film's crew to build camaraderie. This probably wasn't one of those.

I leaned back attempting to escape the effects of the man's tobacco smoke. "Keep talking." He was intentionally trying to rile, so I countered with a deadpan. On me, it's hard to tell the difference.

Ford laughed deep in his throat and then coughed wetly. "I like you, kid. I like damn few people anymore." He pinched the spent tip with his finger, broke it in two— just like Smokey the Bear would have wanted—and dropped it to the floor next to what I now saw was a script for *The Alamo*.

"Like me? You really don't know me."

"I spoke to Bill Donovan this time last year." The smoke curled up his face, around his left eye and dark eye patch, under the lens of his glasses, to lie briefly like fog beneath the bill of his blue ball cap. "He gave me a full report on you. Disney backed it up."

I knew Donovan had been head of the CIA before he'd died last February. And he'd recruited Walt who, in turn, had sort of recruited me. All of which suggested that this inquiry of Ford's might be more than a simple murder investigation.

The director pointed his briarwood at me. "And I understand that you live, eat, and sleep on a boat docked near Santa Monica. Are you a good seaman?"

I considered the western outfit I was wearing. "You think I am a cowboy?"

The director of *Stagecoach*, *The Searchers*, and *Wee Willie Winkie* laughed. "I like that too. Shows spunk and independence. Indicates a—"

"It indicates simple poverty. And maybe a willingness to make a buck honestly."

He clamped his teeth down on his pipe stem and grunted, "Goddamn right. So here's what I need."

The case he wanted me to work had to do with a stabbing death of a Mexican bit player during the filming of John Wayne's *The Alamo* over in Brackettville, near the border. A blonde woman, Lajean Ethridge, stage named Lajean Guye, had been killed early Sunday morning by her boyfriend, Chester Smith.

The day before, Wayne had expanded Ethridge's role in the movie, and she'd thought she was moving up, witnesses said. Smith had thought otherwise and used a five-inch hunting knife to make his point.

The local sheriff had Smith in the hoosegow without bond, pending Grand Jury action for having willfully committed the homicide. The perpetrator claimed to have no memory of the incident, for hours before and after, he'd been found with the victim's bloody corpse. Ford wanted me to go see him.

"What good will that do?"

The director sucked dryly on the pipe. "There's something funny about all this. Duke is involved and I want to know how, before it all comes back to bite him on the ass." He coughed deeply again and spat on the limo's floor, spattering the script. "He's up to his eyebrows in problems and debt with this movie that he's determined to get made. I want the heat kept off him, unless he's absolutely involved."

"Can I talk to Wayne about it?"

"Not without checking first with me." He concentrated on getting his pipe going again and then grumbled, "Rumor has it that this Smith character was hopped up on some new kind of dope. If there's even a ghost of a chance that drugs are associated with this, it can ruin the picture and Duke's reputation. He pinned me with his right eye and breathed pipe-smoke. "So find out, kid, but keep your trap shut around Wayne."

My sinuses were screaming from the blue haze, but I kept my peace. I could tell that Ford enjoyed employing me on the sly, but I decided, then and there, that Wayne needed to know why I was on his movie set, and I needed to keep things open and above board, no matter what Ford wanted.

Over all, it sounded like a routine case of a jealous lover to me. I might be back home in a few days. Smith, who killed the woman, probably couldn't accept the fact that she was fooling around with John Wayne. According to some less-than-reliable sources, Wayne had a thing for Mexican women. He'd even married a couple of them. He was no Errol Flynn, but I knew that whenever he wanted to get away from Hollywood, he'd go down to the "old country" where he could feel like a king.

"I love Duke like a son," Ford told me. "But he's a dumbass businessman. He's like that Welles kid, dying to direct an American classic." The director cleared his throat wetly, and then cleared it again. Maybe he was catching my cold.

"You sound like you're dying a little yourself."

He grunted. "I've damn near caught pneumonia down here. You can tell from the way I'm breathing."

"And smoking."

"I'll have to stay back at the hotel for the next week." He coughed again, as if the thought of his illness caused an involuntary physical reaction. "That's the job I'm hiring you to do, Wade. Do we have a deal?"

The limo slowed and it felt like our discussion was over. I pushed up the brim of my hat with a thumb. "We have a deal, Ford."

"And you're going to have a couple of black eyes."

CHAPTER 3

A few minutes later, Joe joined us and we traveled west on Highway 90 for over an hour from San Antonio, we reached Brackettville, which didn't do much to impress me and I'm sure that the feeling was mutual. We blow through the little town, past the only three two-story buildings on its main drag. I was sure I saw a genuine dry-goods store next to the post office and town hall. The Ranchero nosed north up route 674 several miles to the arid ranch where the movie set had been constructed, according to Joe, to actual scale with actual adobe

All I could think was: "I hope it doesn't rain and become actual mud."

I'd never been in the West before. I'd been to places

like Palm Springs and I'd summered at a dude ranch when I was in my teens, but this…this was Texas, the Real West. Cattle ranches, oil wells, and roundups. Jack rabbits, field sparrows, and dicky birds.

I'd expected lots of romantic expanses like Monument Valley—full of cactus, wild horses, and ghost towns. What I got was scrub, sand, blinding sunlight, and acres of weeds—none of them tumbling.

While Ford turned his full attention back to the script, Joe rolled, lit another smoke, and shook his bushy head. "Wayne has more than a million dollars of his own money sunk into this picture."

"Someday you'll have to show me how to do that," I said, motioning at his cigarette. "I could use it to impress girls."

"I hear it's given him an ulcer."

"Who?"

"Wayne. Who are we talking about?"

I studied my face in the rearview mirror. No doubt about it. I was getting two of the blackest and bruised eyes in the business. "That's show biz, I guess." I went back to gazing out the window at the passing prairie.

Despite the limo's air conditioning, the temperature felt warm and the sky outside the cruising car looked dusty. It got darker and thicker as we neared the move location, seemingly in the middle of nowhere.

Wayne had leased 400 acres of a ranch from someone named, Happy Shanan to create the biggest movie set outside of Hollywood. Heavy construction equipment growled, heaved, and shoved the landscape as we rolled to a stop. The construction reminded me of places I'd been months earlier during the expansion of Disneyland and the new Dodger Stadium site, only here there were horses, cows, and a few roaming chickens.

Joe and I descended from Ford's oddball station wagon and wandered, almost getting trampled by a mini-stampede of longhorn cattle. I asked why Wayne wanted to shoot in this god-forsaken location in west Texas.

"He wanted to do it in Mexico." Joe sidestepped a cow paddy. "It's cheaper there, but the DAR said they'd never let him live it down. And there's no way to film at the actual Alamo in downtown San Antonio, so—"

A breeze caught the edge of my hat, and I laid a hand on my crown, pushing it down a tad, which made my dark forehead ache more. "Why's he even making this movie? Everyone identifies Fess Parker with Davy Crockett. It's almost an act of Congress."

Joe waved off into the distance at Frankie Avalon, who was dress in buckskins and long hair. "I think he remembers another picture he was in with Robert Montgomery."

"*They Were Expendable*. Ford directed that one."

"Yep. And I think, in Wayne's view, the Alamo was a holding action until Sam Houston could get his act together against the Mexicans."

Interesting.

"So Davy, Travis, Bowie, and the others were expendables. And this movie is Wayne's way of responding to Ford's earlier picture."

"Well, I wouldn't go that far. But it's been my experience that all actors what to direct. They're crazy that way."

"Most people think stuntmen are the crazy ones."

Joe just grinned and we kept walking.

The film had been beset with setbacks. Aside from the murder and a heavy rainstorm that had softened the adobe walls to sludge in places, a herd of longhorns had gotten lose from their corral and trampled the set, injuring a couple of extras. Then there had been a locust storm recently, considered by many here as a bad omen. Canutt observed that the grasshopper still lies heavy, casting an air of depression on the overworked movie company.

The set was a lot like the rodeo had been, but it was more organized and as compact as a military camp. Longhorn steers were corralled off to the east of the main compound. A fleet of trucks and camera vehicles circulated between the makeshift housing for the crew and authentic adobe walls that encircled the movie's open-air set.

Ford caught my eye, yelled my name for all to hear, and waved me over to a flapping tent that could have housed Sam Houston's entire staff. Inside, I found a series of camp chairs and folding tables that served as an office for today's activities. There, I also found John

Wayne, mopping his bald head with a towel labeled *Property of Hotel Austin.*

He was dragging on a Lucky Strike and studying a chessboard. A cute but tired script girl stood at his side, holding a sweating glass of iced tea or whiskey in one hand and a series of pink typed script pages in the other. Wayne wrinkled his brow and smacked her on the rump. Then he took a long pull on the contents of the glass. I could hear ice tinkle and smell that it wasn't tea, once he gave me his full attention.

"So you're the private eye that Pappy's saddled me with, are you?" He indicated a steamer trunk next to a ham radio setup. "I love him like a father, but he's a terrible bully. Set'er down there, son."

A lot of people had strong opinions about Wayne. Some thought he was a wooden oaf. Others that he was an American icon. Still others believed he was an average actor who lucked out from stuntman to B-westerns to A-westerns.

I remembered seeing him on the silver screen when I was a kid. There had been a couple of serials with him in them and the *Three Mesquiteers* series of movies. During the war, I'd watched him fight the Japs and later, with Ford's help, fight the Apaches.

The movies he appeared in were usually pretty good, but his performance seemed wooden in most. Maybe that was the plan all along, to portray the average guy a little awkwardly and thus connect with the audience. He'd connected with me only twice—once in the boxing scene of *The Quiet Man* and, once again, whistling at the end of *The High and the Mighty*. Taken together, Wayne's movie image was "quiet and mighty." I'd never realized that before this moment, and it struck me like lightning, but I didn't let it show.

"No thanks, I'll stand."

I learned a longtime ago that I'd get further with most Hollywood types by suppressing my boyish charm, such as it is. Acting hard-boiled was a cliché, but movie people expected it from a private eye. Cops, however, hated it, but knowing the correct stance to take often was half my profession. Sort of like method acting.

"Oh, you will, will you?" Wayne glared. "Around here, you'll do as I say, or you're out. Fast."

He was playing the role of the bullheaded movie controller, but I wouldn't give him the upper hand. "That'll be the day."

Wayne's expression softened when he heard the familiar phrase from his *Hondo* movie. He made a V with the fingers of one hand and pointed them at the bridge of his nose. "Where'd you get those shiners?"

I told him that I walked into a couple of doors, and he smirked, leaning to one side. I didn't know what he was about to say in response since we were interrupted by the entrance through the tent flap of the meanest-looking man I'd ever met. The script girl actually gasped and took a step back.

Wayne set his glass down and shook the man's hand. They both grunted and appeared to be playing at some sort of test of strength, possibly for my benefit. "Slate, you should meet our new man, here. Says he's a detective. Name of Stan Wade."

The Slate character gave me a what-do-you-take-me-for look. "Right. And my name is Phyllis Marlowe."

I smiled and let him pull my leg, sort of.

Slate extended the same hand he's just given Wayne. I thought I recognized him as the guy who was breathing fire back at the rodeo. The handshake was indeed a true test of strength. I lost, but again I tried not to show it. "What's your real name?"

"Toriano. Men call me Firewrangler."

My eyebrows went up before I could stop them. "And you made fun of my name."

I had a couple of scars on me, but *this* guy was like a living cicatrix. My guess was that he'd been in numerous knife fights, or else he'd cut himself to prove that he was alive. They said some people did that. His skin gleamed with a series of crisscrossed raised lines, like a series of combat medals. His eyes were the reddest I'd ever seen, and that was when he was in a good mood. His teeth seemed ten percent larger than they should have been. And he had a tendency to growl when he spoke.

"I want you two to work together on this," Wayne ordered.

It was hard to tell him that I usually worked alone. It

was also untrue. But I didn't like letting him have the upper hand.

I didn't care for Slate at all. He looked like the kind of guy who'd licked everyone in the county, including cripples. He was of a type I'd encountered several times before, starting back when I was a kid at a dude ranch. Someone who looked and acted strange and thought he owned the world. I later learned that he was a seminal-black—part Indian and part Negro. A descendent of what was known as the Buffalo Soldiers of the 1880s. He was proud, confident, and a little too authoritative for my taste. But there seemed to be a dark-yet-soft-inner self hidden beneath his tough, reddish exterior. Kinda like a Tootsie-Roll Pop.

I used to know a guy like him. He got drunk and fell off his boat one night a couple of miles out in the bay and was never recovered. I liked to think that he was still alive and kicking somewhere, but doubted it.

I raised an open palm in protest. "Hold on a minute. That's not the way I like to work."

"Well, that's the way you're gonna work, Mister Detective." The Duke went back to studying the chessboard. "Slate knows his way around. Now, get going. I don't want to be bothered by this mess again until it's cleared up."

If it had been anyone else, I would have argued, but at the moment it didn't seem worth the effort. So I figured that Mister Firewrangler would be my faithful Indian companion and native guide wrapped into one. From his point of view, I was probably just another stupid White man.

As we ducked out of the tent, the brim of my hat caught the pole and canted sideways. "Looks better that way," Wayne called out.

I straightened it casually, feeling like a cross between Pat Butrum and Pat Brady.

Slate didn't say a word. Nonetheless, we were now partners of a sort in the investigation of the blonde actress's murder, whether I liked it or not. I immediately started thinking of ways to get rid of him. Short of murder.

CHAPTER 4

Since my cold was still hanging on, I went to a Brackettville motel room early and soaked my head with cold wet towel after a supper of hot, spicy chili. The premiere of something called "The Untouchable" came on a snowy TV, but I drifted off to a peaceful sleep and didn't see the end.

In the morning, the facts as I learned them were that the previous Sunday, around two a.m., Sheriff John Sheedy had charged slender, dark-haired Chester Harvey Smith, thirty-two, with the homicide of LaJean Ethridge, about twenty-six, who used the professional name of LaJean Guye. Smith had confessed, but appeared to be in limited mental state when found with the body and the bloody knife.

"A crime of passion and professional jealousy," Smith's lawyer, Fred Samaan, called it, but rumor had it that Wayne was somehow involved. The Duke didn't have time to testify during what would surely become a circus of a trial, full of bad publicity for his movie. But the local press was already describing the murder weapon as a Bowie knife from the film set.

Slate and I got permission to interview Smith in a cramped room at the back of the Brackettville Police station where he was "sobering up." We waited patiently until an overweight deputy with catsup stains on his shirt front brought in the prisoner.

Chet Smith was a lean, strung-out man with a thin beard and high forehead under dark, unruly locks. He reminded me of John Carradine. He was sweating from the heat, and his circumstances, as his deputy/guard brought him in cuffed and seated him in a metal folding chair across the table from us. Seated there across from us in handcuffs, he seemed groggy and unsure of what was happening.

"I don't remember anything about it."

Smith stared at Slate and me, focusing on us for the first time. There was a question in his expression. "Holy Mackerel, Andy. Are—are you the Lone Ranger? And Tonto?"

I looked at Slate, who barked, "Don't let my partner's black eyes fool you. I'm the one in charge here."

I disagreed, but didn't comment. We were having

enough trouble communicating with this guy and didn't need to argue authority—at least, for the moment.

Smith licked his dry lips and asked for a cigarette.

I glanced at the guard who shook his head with undisguised distain. In my experience, most cops felt that way about me, or maybe it was the company I was currently keeping.

Smith was having trouble focusing on us. "The Chinaman usually gets them for me, but he refused."

Slate leaned in with interest. "What Chinaman?"

"You know—the guy who was just here."

Now, I too was interested and glanced around to see if anyone else was nearby. "What guy?"

"Guy, you know?" Smith's palms left damp streaks on the worn table's surface.

"What guy?"

"That's his name. Guy."

Slate was becoming impatient. He clinched his hands. "A Chinese guy named Guy?"

I got out a notebook. Lately my memory had been playing tricks on me, so I'd taken to writing down these sorts of loose details. "What's this guy's last name?"

Smith stared at me and cocked his head. "Wong."

I closed the notebook. "Third base."

The guard moved in closer to us. "No. Smitty's right. The man who interviewed him just before you two came in was called Guy Wong, but he's no Chinaman. He was the tall…uh…fellow you passed on your way in."

Smith sat back in satisfaction at having been proven right. "Keeps his cigarettes in an elephant."

We all stared at the prisoner dumbly.

Then the guard shoved the bill of his cap back with his thumb. "He means envelope. The guy, Wong, carried his smokes in an envelope."

Slate glared at the guard. "Yeah, we got that."

I, too, looked at the guard. Hard. "And you didn't think that was suspicious?"

"I didn't let him give him any." He gestured the thumb at Smith. "That's why he's asking you for a smoke."

Slate got to his feet. "I think we need to have a talk with this—"

I didn't let him finish. "Yep, I agree."

We headed back out the door together as Smith's voice came from behind us. "I'm going away soon, ain't I?"

"Smitty," the guard answered, "you're already on a long trip."

⌖

"Gimme the catsup, Wade."

We sat at the lunch counter with the overweight deputy, who ate a double cheeseburger in big bites.

I slid the plastic squeeze bottle his way. "You know how you can tell a cop?"

He swallowed. "Tell a cop what?"

"It's in the eyebrows. When something strange happens, a normal person's eyebrows go up in surprise."

He licked the corner of his mouth. "Yeah?"

Slate spoke in a soft drawl. "But cop's eyebrows go down, 'cause he's interested."

The deputy burped quietly, eyebrows steady, and jerked his chin at a dark figure of a man passing beyond the plate glass window. "That's him."

Out in the shade of a hardware store's tattered awing across the street, the dark figure tried to look in our direction from the reflection of the shop's display window.

Slate swiveled on his lunch-counter stool. "And he's watching us."

I tossed some change on the counter. "Let's go see what he wants."

The deputy stayed put. "So you're saying that cops aren't normal people."

I got up and patted him on the shoulder. "Don't let it bother you."

Out in the glare of the noon-day sun, I saw the dark man climb into a late-model Buick. Slate and I double-timed it to our jeep, intending to follow.

Even though we were in a rush, my tough-guy partner started giving me background on our quarry, while using the vehicle's cigarette lighter to fire up a Camel. Since we were meandering through light traffic, intent on not being spotted, there was nothing I could do but sit back, inhale the scent of his smoke, and listen as Slate began by telling me that the dark man couldn't really be called Guy Wong.

I steered around a paperboy wobbling on his bike. "How do you know that?"

He planted the heels of his boots on the jeep's scared dash and leaned back with a faint smile. "My mother gave me the name Firewrangler. We were with the Trailville Circus, back in the late Twenties, before the Depression."

"Get real," I challenged, but he ignored the comment and flicked ashes at a Stop sign as the Buick turned left in front of us, past a tiny theater showing *Francis Joins the WACS*. "So, you know this Guy, guy?"

The answer came quick. "Known him from six months ago. We were employed in an operation bringing contraband across the border into the States. Wong would hand off the 'goods' to me near some small desert crossing town, and then we'd both get paid on our respective sides of the border by exchanging drop locations."

I turned left out of the commercial district, sneezed from the smoke or my cold, and scanned for the Buick among the small residential lots and cross streets.

"The man who ran the operation gave us each other's payoff location. When we met, we'd swap goods and info at the same time. I'd tell him where he could get paid down in Piedras Negras and he'd tell me—"

"I know. He'd tell you where to go." I thought I saw the Buick, so I sped up and made a right.

Slate sat up in his seat, peering ahead. "Where'd that car go? Did you lose him?"

"I didn't lose him. He probably spotted us and is doubling back. What were the goods you were bringing across the border?"

"Chinks."

I shot him a glance of disbelief. "Chinks? You mean Chinese people?"

"That's the one group of illegal's who want to get into this country more than Mexicans. They've got plenty of money to do it, too." He leaned back and tossed his cigarette at a passing mailbox. "And you lost him, Kimo."

I clinched my jaw, which made my forehead hurt even more. "Great balls of fire."

CHAPTER 5

I circled the block. "It's just like Jerry Lee Lewis says."

"Jerry Lewis, the spastic actor?" Slate asked.

"Jerry *Lee* Lewis, the—the singer. You of all people should appreciate this." I was hoping to distract him from my apparent surveillance error.

"So what does he say?"

"Goodness, gracious, great balls of fire."

I should have known that Slate wouldn't get my musical reference, but I was sort of desperate. He stared intently down an alley. "For white guy, you're not very funny."

"And for a…oh, forget it. Let's get out of here.

There was nothing left to do but go report back to Wayne and Ford.

こうこう

Wayne's hair seemed to change from dark black to gray, depending on the light and toupee. "This damn picture is like *Hondo* all over again, only worse."

Ford ran a pipe cleaner through the barrel of his briarwood. "At least you're not shooting it in three-D."

Wayne ignored the verbal jab and studied Slate and me. "So who is this guy, again?"

The black Indian explained how our quarry had been, and probably still was, the source of mind-altering drug coming across the border to the site of Duke's movie. "There are hundreds of these coyotes employed by you as cheap labor. Imagine—if even one of them were a carrier of smallpox or something worse…"

We were inside a Wayne's "Command Center," a decked out, silver motor home joined to a construction site trailer. Some of us were standing, some sitting all worried and on edge.

"What's worse than smallpox?" I wondered aloud.

"Anything even mildly contagious that causes men to see insane visions and commit murder."

"We've got to do something to stop it." Wayne's voice sounded bit like a rusty hinge. "A thing like that could put a permanent end to filming, not to mention the effect it might have on the average citizen if it got loose."

"The best way to stop it is at the source. There's a clinic down in Cuadid Acuna, run by a Doctor Zachariah Cortina. We should investigate."

Ford rammed the pipe cleaner through one last time. "You ought to get Ward to be in this picture."

I wondered if the old director had even been listening.

"I asked him. He's busy with that *Wagon Train* TV series."

Ford thumbed tobacco from a leather pouch into the bowl of his pipe. "Then get McLaglen."

"You know that Vic is near death. Give us all a break, Pappy, and let me handle this thing."

The phone started ringing. Wayne picked up the receiver then slammed it back down without a word.

Slate persisted, jerking a thumb in my direction. "The black-eyed private eye here could go down across the border and check things out for you."

My back stiffened. I wondered what all the sane people were doing that evening.

"This location is too flat for good cinema." Ford tried to get his opinions in around our discussion. "It's a lousy background. You need something like Monument Valley."

Wayne turned to him. "I'm not like Dick Powell, Coach, just another actor who wants to direct. You know that, so stop messing with my movie."

"I will the hell not. I made you what you are today, you hard-nosed son of a bitch, but I'm beginning to feel like Doctor Frankenstein." The elder director struck fire to his pipe. "And remember, I know that you profited by staying out of World War II." Ford directed his attention to me. "He thinks I'm butting in on his pet movie. But he forgets that he did the exact same thing to Boetticher ten years ago. The definition of a director is that he's a man who has the balls to butt in."

The ole man chuckled at his own inadvertent joke. Or maybe it hadn't been inadvertent and he was just acting. I honestly couldn't tell. Maybe they both were.

Wayne looked disgusted, like he'd swallowed too much rotgut. "Are you going to throw WW Two at me again? Republic and I had an advantage then and used it to get ahead, but if we hadn't, you never would have been able to get that studio to make your pet project, *The Quiet Man*, so we're even and don't bring it up again."

Ford cleared his throat, possibly to hold his audience's attention. "I've got six Oscars."

"And none of them for a western. This is a big movie about a place that Americans can still go and see today, back in San Antone. I'm not directing some fantasy here."

The air around Ford was thick like that of a small forest fire.

I tried diplomacy. "Gentlemen, are we going to do anything about this Doctor Zachariah, or just let nature take its un-natural course?" Out of the edge of my eye, I could see Slate smile and chew on a toothpick.

Wayne spat, then remembered where he was. "Christ! Let's not go off half-cocked. I've got an arrangement with the Mexican authorities who can look into this. I can check in with Rodriquez and—"

"It won't take but a few hours for the Fireman and me to go check into this medical clinic," I said.

The toothpick froze in the side of Slate's mouth.

Wayne thought for a long moment, and we all waited in the rare silence. Finally he agreed, telling us that he'd make arrangements for us to cross the border and that we were to just look around, stay out of trouble, and be sure that the jeep had a full tank of gas.

That sounded reasonable to me, and it would give me a chance to show Slate that a good PI was better at tracking than a bad scout was.

As we were leaving, Ford's gravelly voice rang out again. "And you should add a scene where you light your smoke from the stack of a kerosene lamp."

"We've done that in four other pictures, Pappy," Wayne came back, and the phone began ringing again. "But I'll see that it's added to the script somewhere. Will that satisfy you?"

"Always a classic."

오오

Brackettville was only three miles east of the border. It was hard to believe that we were across the Del Rio River now. I wondered if it would be this easy coming back.

I still had on the remains of my rodeo outfit, but Slate—

The Firewrangler was decked out for a journey into the old west. He wore a military revolver holstered low on his right hip, a full cartridge band, and campaign hat, soiled with sweat. Riding boots, knee high. Epilated shirt with sleeves rolled to the elbows. He looked like Gilbert Roland with that red-checkered bandanna tied loosely around his neck, double-buckled leather wrist bands, and a set of spurs that did a convincing imitation of hammered gold. "You planning to punch some senoritas or kiss some cows?" he grunted, rotating a toothpick from one side of his whiskered mouth to the other.

I wiped my dripping brow and tried to think of something tough to say, possibly to impress him. We were still measuring each other, sizing one another up while taking in the scorching sunlight.

After another ten minutes driving down Route 54 in the Nava Municipality, Slade commented that the right rear tire was losing air. I reluctantly agreed that he was right. We got out and spent a good ten minutes changing to the spare.

A huge fast-moving shadow passed overhead. I glanced up but could see nothing at first. Then I caught sight of the bird and felt the hair rising under my hat.

It was black as midnight with a naked head and a wingspan over ten feet. It sailed low over us, on rigid wings, covering us again with its shadow.

I instantly shielded my eyes. "Turkey buzzard?"

"That's a condor." Slate's vice was almost a whisper as the bird glided back.

It was awe-inspiring. The creature made low turns over us again. Once I caught a glimpse of its merciless eyes. Then it flew off across an abyss and disappeared below.

The spare tire too seemed a little soft to me, and I figured I might have to go some pumping soon if we didn't find a service station "down Mexico way."

Slate held his hand up to the horizon, palm open toward him, and estimated that the sun would be setting in about an hour. My brother's watch made that to be about six-thirty. Did they observe daylight-savings time in Mexico?

CHAPTER 6

I found the country to be like a cast-off slum. American goods could be found here, but they were dented, ancient, patched, rickety, and faded by the sun. I used to think that Mexicans didn't take care of their things, but I'd since learned that the people didn't have a lot of things to take care of to begin with. And the few they had were protected and treasured, sometimes for generations.

Over here, south of the border, there probably were a few Mexicans who didn't want the Alamo movie to be made. Instead, they likely wanted to re-do the battle and the ones that followed, in order to take back the land for their country.

We continued driving along the dusty road beside a

set of railroad tracks that led into the town proper. My sinuses reacted, commanding me to sneeze from the dirt cloud four times without restraint. Slate shook his head and gave me a disdainful "Jesus" look. High above, a lonely, single-engine airplane droned toward the western sun.

Ciudad Acuna was a ramshackle collection of buildings, thrown together around a central plaza, and a cathedral. It impressed me more than Brackettville had. The plaza was still the main social gathering place for the town's residents, with small shops, a stand where you could get a shoeshine, and a few rusty autos parked near a cantina called Ma Crosby's. Slate knew the bar as "the best joint in town" to get margaritas, mariachi music, and information.

We strolled casually inside. I tipped my hat to the rotund barkeep the way Randolph Scott would have. "Nice little town you've got here."

The man flicked a short cloth at a fly on the bar and then gestured grandly for us to have a seat at a table near a smoke-streaked stone fireplace.

I discovered that I was starving and joined Slate in ordering the *especial del dia*. There was a tender, smoky *cabrito*—roasted young goat—served with a half onion, roasted, and camarones Crosby, which I found were shrimp stuffed with cheese and peppers wrapped in bacon.

Surprisingly, I was delighted to find that I could

wash it all down with a tall glass of cherry Kool-Aid. "What does a Firewrangler do, exactly?"

Slate eyed me and my drink. "He flourishes the flames."

I thought he winked. "And people pay good money for that?"

"Bet on it, Pard." He twitched a finger at my glass. "And by the way, that stuff makes you look like you're wearing lipstick."

I chomped on a red pepper, hoping it would make my complexion blend in with my lips.

My silent partner sat drinking a beer, absently digging at the cork on the underside of the bottle cap with his thumb nail.

I remained calm, quiet, and deliberate, which was getting us nowhere at the speed of light.

Since we had the place to ourselves, except for a drunk sleeping on crossed arms at the end of the bar, I decided to take the metaphorical bull by the horns and asked the barkeep for directions to Dr. Z's clinic.

"The Saint Anthony Hospital is down Hidalgo road, *senors*. Turn right at Allende." He waved a damp towel in a westerly direction. "Across the bridge on Mateos highway, near the dam."

"We'll find it," Slate growled, standing and leaving a crumpled ten-dollar bill on the table. "You forget, Wade. I've been there before."

Outside and to the east, the sky was turning lavender

and deep blue. A few early stars were showing. "The sky really does turn purple at twilight out here," I said.

I wondered what caused it. Norman would know the scientific reason. I'd have to ask him—if I got back.

തരൗ

It was full dark as we motored slowly past a few houses, scattered outside of town like a handful of dusty dice. As we neared a low building set back from the road, I saw a hand-carved sign swinging on simple door hinges, informing us that this was the St. Anthony Clinic.

Slate shut off the engine, and we coasted over popping gravel. As we rolled to a complete stop, the silence of the night became populated with the sounds of crickets, a distant coyote, and the tiny tones of a cornet rippling from a radio somewhere inside the single-story medical facility. At night, the lonely place did little to encourage thoughts of health and wellness. I made a mental bet with myself that the majority of the operations performed here were abortions.

I figured that we had done enough now, having located the Chinese guy and Dr. Z. We could come back in the morning or send someone else to investigate. But the Wrangler of Fire had other ideas. "Let's move."

"Let's not."

"We're here."

"We're leaving."

"I'm driving."

"Pretty soon, you'll be walking."

"Try it, cowpoke, and you'll be on your ass." He got out and let the driver-side door click quietly shut, while pocketing the ring of keys.

This would've been an excellent time to have a gun. Since this was to have been a simple reconnaissance mission, mine was still in my suitcase back in Brackettville. In lieu of any other weapon, I picked up a soft-ball sized rock and hefted it as we crouched nearer to the darkened side of the facility. Brambles crunched beneath our boots, sounding to me like gun shots. Something small in the bush scampered away in fear. I didn't blame it.

We came up on the building from the rear, where pale light poured from a pair of dingy windows. I was hoping for a storeroom or maybe a kitchen, but what I saw through the semi-clouded glass was more like a mad laboratory from a cheapie monster movie.

The interior walls of the room were white porcelain blocks and the floor was gray linoleum tile. A row of lift-top freezes ran along one side of the room and a black countertop complete with dripping faucet and steel sink stretched along another wall. On the countertop were beakers, test-tube racks, a microscope, and one of those centrifuges, spinning a humming like a child's top. As research labs went, CalTech probably wasn't as well equipped as this place.

On a file cabinet next to an exam table sat a device

that churned out a strip of paper covered with squiggles. The operating table, itself, was in the center of the room under a cantilevered lamp, and it cradled a dark-haired oriental woman, asleep or dead, legs held high and wide in metal stirrups, under a light blue sheet.

Slate growled deep in his throat like an anxious junkyard dog.

I thought he was going to sniff the air. "So, where's this Dr. Z?"

"Right behind you, gentlemen. Turn around slowly, or my bodyguard will shoot you as the trespassers that you are."

Yep, real nice town.

୧୨୧

"Oh, hey there. No need to get excited." I grinned like a Hollywood charmer, which was sort of true. "I'm Jimmy Joe Meeker from up Houston way. Oil's my business. Do you know your place is sitting on one of the finest deposits of natural crude within four hundred miles?"

I offered a friendly hand, hoping the guy wearing the white lab coat would take it. He also wore a slim, oddly handsome face with thinning, slicked back hair and a pair of wire-rimmed glasses over a straight nose. His shoulders were trim compared to the burly man beside him wearing the gun.

Both men took instead a step back as I ambled farther into the faint square of light from the barely translucent windows. That's when the gun guy started firing.

I ducked at the sight of the muzzle flash and heard another shot fired over my head from behind me. Slate had gotten his gun out, but it went spinning from his hand, struck by the other man's bullet, the same way I'd seen happen in countless westerns.

All the night sounds of nature stopped, waiting for our next move.

I slowly rose. "Ah, that's damn fine shooting."

Slate was holding his right hand in his left, letting the blood trickle from and between his fingers. I'd half suspected that my faithful companion had led me here—a lamb to slaughter, but now that idea had been proven false.

Lab Coat moved in closer to the light, and I could see the hard expression in his flinty eyes. "Turn around. Both of you."

I couldn't stop myself from moaning slightly, knowing what probably came next.

I was right. Something solid struck the lower right side of my head and I struck the dark Mexican soil.

Vaya con Dios.

CHAPTER 7

Yeah, the black-and-white clown was tap-dancing on my head again. He was wearing a broad grin and a baseball uniform. There was a crystal ball setting on a little table and he put his palms out toward it as if to warm his hands in its glow.

I awoke to find the blurry face of an angel hovering above me in a similar glow. I knew she was an angel because of her white halo. I blinked hard and the angel smiled and moved away. She came back a second later, her dark hair crowned with a nurse's cap, instead of a halo. The nurse smiled again with wet lips and placed a cold compress on my forehead. I blessed her for it. She quietly laughed and spoke with a mild South American accent. "I will help you, if you will help me."

This struck me as a pretty good deal under the circumstances. Her dark eyes held mine in earnest. I read in them a host of fear, doubt, and a hint of panic. What happened to the angelic smile?

I elbowed myself up into a sitting position. "You bet."

The sound of approaching footsteps made her eyes flash and my heart jump. She pushed me down and placed a finger across her lips to indicate silence.

I slid back down and closed my eyes, playing along.

"You were not supposed to touch him, Rosita," a man's deep voice warned.

Then I heard the unmistakable sound of a slap, followed immediately by a whimper.

I could crack my eyes open enough in the muted light to see the fallen angel crouched there at the man's feet. His hand came back to her hard again, this time stroking her dark glossy hair. His legs moved away. She looked at me with wet eyes and shook her head, "No."

I got up anyway, dammit, on the wrong side of rage.

That's when I saw the other beds and the woman out cold in them. Individual IV bags were slowly dripping above each of them. There was a man standing at the farthest bed. It was the Chinese guy, still holding his gun and he was standing over the prone figure of Slate, also unconscious and absorbing the liquid feed from a suspended bag.

"What the hell is all this?" I discovered that I was restrained by a leather strap connecting my right wrist to the bed frame. "Why are those women here?"

Dr. Z came over and tightened a restraint on my left wrist, giving me no alternative but to lie back down. He flashed a light into my eyes and nodded. "They are indigent Orientals who came requesting medical relief."

"But you gave them so much more," I deadpanned.

He slid the penlight into a pocket of his hospital gown.

I had a pretty good idea what was happening now. "You've infected them—with something that makes them crazy, like Smith."

The nurse...what was her name?...Rosita...came over to stand at the doctor's side, who gestured with an open hand at the row of beds and their dozing occupants. "Ah, Smith was a test that proved that the hallucinogenic virus survives in males, as well as females. These subjects are the valiant carriers of Mexico's future."

I didn't have a pretty good idea of what was happening anymore, and it must have shown on my face.

The doctor's calm features included a set of perfectly aligned and impressively white teeth. "These woman and others like them will cross the border and within days will spread confusion and uncertainty throughout the southwestern United States. And within weeks, Mexico will be able to re-acquire the territory it lost decades ago to the USA."

His cultured voice carried not a bit of Latin American accent. His warm breath was as fresh as a florists shop. "We will simply walk right in and no one will care, because the military, the government, and even the lowly citizens of your country will be gone, gone out of their minds, into a fantasy land of idiot dreams. Understand?"

This sounded so bizarre that, for a moment, I thought that I was still dreaming. Or maybe Ford and Wayne had staged all this as a joke on the new guy.

Then the angelic Rosita gave the doctor a hug and handed him a syringe.

The words tumbled out of my mouth in a panic. "Wait. You mean that you've infected these people for the sake of some grand political vision? And the Alamo is the center of your strategy?"

"Hmmm. You have a sharp mind, Mr. Wade. Let me tell you about the Alamo."

"Okay," I said, drawing out the word.

"You Americans like to talk about the 150 or so proud defenders who died there, but more than 1,500 Mexican troops were killed at the siege of that godforsaken place. And the majority of the people inside the Alamo weren't Americans at all. They were from foreign countries, including Mexico."

I slowly strained to try to work my wrist free, but no luck. "Yes, but why some sick disease?"

The lenses of his glasses caught the light and flashed as he studied the syringe. "To make life easier for all on both sides of the border. Soon you arrogant Americans will simply lie down and give everything back to the Beaners, Breeds, Chicanos, and Wetbacks. This is not some sick disease, this is heroin, or 'snow' laced with a form of lysergic acid. The researchers at your Battelle Institute in Ohio wrote a paper on its effects to nullify military troops so that an invader could easily take over without a fight."

"Cards on the table," I said. "Are you a real doctor?"

Rosita stood next to a steaming autoclave, her face filled with concern. Zachariah Cortina, if that was his real name, stared at me. "Oh, yes. I've had medical training, complements of your US Navy, in fact. My brother worked in a small shop in Tijuana, selling trinkets and jumping beans to tourists. He was unjustly accused of picking the pocket of an American visiting from San Diego. The tourist's father was some high official who, as you say, had the book thrown at my brother.

"He was sentenced to five years in prison where he worked on a gang digging a trench almost by hand so that the town's sewage would drain in the direction of Baja. He came down with a terrible disease and I happened to be called in to treat him."

Rosita was trying to signal something from behind the man's back. Her longish nose and short upper lip showed off her delicate smile.

The doctor sighed. "I wanted to move him to my clinic, but his pain was so great that he tried to hang himself. I discovered a way to deaden his pain...at a cost. He called to me one night, screaming for relief. There was no way to help him, except to inject him with this serum. I watched him calmly wither away and vowed revenge on the savage white men who had transformed my brother into a sick suffering animal."

I could only think of one thing to say to all of that. "What a cliché!"

Yet, of the entire story, I was most surprised that, in this day and age, he considered people like me as "White men." One of us needed their thinking updated. I hoped it wasn't me.

I'd been playing for time, of course. The look on the doctor's face told me that he'd known it all along. "We act like we control our lives, but we don't."

"With germ warfare?"

"Nothing so primitive. My 'treatment' is a designed drug that will cure a terrible condition which has gone on for far too long. People are suffering and ethics will do nothing to help them. Medical science stopped polio and gave the treatment to every child in your country, as if it were the law. But it took a dying president and a March of Dimes to do it. Nobody cares to cure cycle cell anemia in Negroes yet, or autism, or Parkinson's disease. But now they will. Now, when the threat becomes big enough. In order to save all those who suffer, I'm making the threat big enough to demand notice."

I realized that any further arguments would only make things worse. I began imagining that this was possibly the end. The thought stiffened every muscle in my body.

The Chinese Guy came into view. He whispered something to the mad doctor. Something containing the words, "boss" and "problem."

Dr. Z rested a hand gently on the other man's forearm. Rosita stepped between them. The doctor shook his head reluctantly. "All right. You handle it, and I'll get things together."

Rosita remained silent, but her eyes searched back at me.

The Gun Guy spun his weapon in his huge hand and brought the butt end down hard on my crown. Too late, I called out, "Cliché," as my entire head and everything else went black, just like my eyes.

CHAPTER 8

The clown rode by on a pony with a dog on his shoulders. All three were wearing baseball uniforms. Yeah, it was worse than I'd imagined. My hat was gone and my head almost with it.

I'd been captured and trussed up half-a-dozen times in the last year by various creeps and bad guys, but this man demonstrated maniacal intent more than anyone I'd ever encountered.

I came too gradually, sluggishly, wishing I were back on my boat in LA. Slate and I were trussed up with surgical tape and dumped into the trunk of the body-guard's Buick. I caught a glimpse of Nurse Angel as the lid slammed shut. She appeared to be saying one word over and over, "Pray. Pray."

The air was close in the dark space, and I'd been struck in the head too often. The car started up, and we bumped over a curb or pothole. My forehead smacked into the base of the tire jack. And I saw the clown looking down mockingly before he turned into an Indian chief, trailing a tail of black buzzard feathers.

∾∽∾

Something didn't smell tight. In fact, it smelled rotten. I sniffed through my congestion and knew immediately that the stink was a combination of leaking gasoline and my friend, the Firewrangler.

Slate was still out cold, but that didn't stop him from passing gas. A feeling of dread and a little anger came over me. If he didn't wake up, I didn't know what I'd do with his limp body.

Whatever they administered to him from that dripping bag had put him under, into a deep slumber. I regretted thinking that. A coma is nothing to kid about.

I nudged his head with my knee, called his name, and even got an arm around and pinched his left ear lobe with my thumbnail. He was out cold, but breathing regular. I felt a thread of his saliva dribble from the corner of his mouth, but his body was dead weight against and partly atop mine. I had a contingency plan for situations like this, but I couldn't reach the tiny blade I kept taped to the back of my brother's watch.

It was frustrating as hell, disappointing, and a little shameful. I gnawed at the white gummy tape binding my wrists. In my profession, I was accustomed to being captured and hogtied, but this time there was a strong lurking fear that I could soon be dead.

Frustrating to think that I had again put myself in this dangerous situation. I must have a death wish! Disappointing that there was nothing I could do, having gone along with Slate's plan, rather than taking charge, like a trained professional. Shameful that I'd failed and been so goddamn stupid yet again. But on top of it all, I was chillingly frightened that, this time, I wouldn't get away. This time, I could see myself dying. This time, I'd be helpless to stop someone intentionally taking my life.

All that was left was to scream, and squirm, and kick, and run.

Then I calmed down, wondering what Mr. P, my mentor at the agency, would do in a situation like this? The Old Man had taught me to wait it out. There was nothing to be gained in panic. "It's just like being on stakeout, only your options are limited."

Yeah, too limited. I had to whiz like a racehorse.

When the trunk lid sprang open, I knew they would pull me out and probably shoot me on the spot. As expected, the Chinese guy yanked Slate's limp form from off top of me and then his massive hands reached in to pull at my hair and clothes.

I tumbled out onto the ground, grasping a tire iron

that was immediately kicked from my hands. I heard myself whimper as the guy stepped back and his right foot swung away in preparation of kicking at my face. The heavy boot struck near my windpipe. I twisted to one side, coughing with fear and pain. I came to my knees with my hands full of soft, fine dirt that I tried to throw at my attacker's face. He ducked instinctively and that was my cue to lunge off the side of the Buick and dash through the shrubs, stumbling down a rocky slope.

As soon as I caught my full balance, I fell over another slope, came back up, and pounded my legs for what seemed like a steady half hour. When I ran out of breath and staggered to a halt, I was alone in the middle of Mexican Nowhere. I twisted my hands free of their bindings and soon took a long luxurious piss.

The air was crisp. My back and shoulders ached. Something buzzed around my face and then was gone. Insects, bats, or my overworked imagination. I simply didn't know.

Morning took forever to come. The night sky gradually grew gray then rosy, and the sun broke through a wave of white clouds like the yoke of an egg. Soon the air would feel as hot as the coils of a baker's oven. My mind was focused on food, apparently.

I'd seen the wavering heat lines on flat desert highways off in the distance when I'd driven to Muroc or Palm Springs. In those instances, I called the rippling optical effect a mirage. I'd even seen ghostly upside-down ships hanging in the sky above the ocean when I sailed my cabin cruiser, the *Cervantes II*, far into the Pacific. Called that a mirage, too.

I'd *never* seen a mirage before that contained moving people, or one that had a skyline and passing vehicles on both the land and in the air. This new version had music and the faint sounds of traffic—or was I now completely nuts? No, it was a lonely train whistle in the distance, far behind me.

I carefully edged forward, afraid that I might spook it like a wounded deer. I didn't want it to vanish as I neared closer. Faint trails of smoke or dust wafted through it as I got nearer. A keen wind pushed at my body from the left and that's when I knew there was a storm approaching. A storm, not of rain or lightning, but of grit and dirt. The clouds of billowing dust enveloped me, penetrating my eyes and then my throat. The wind increased and the sand tore at me, knocking me off my feet. My shirt wrapped around my head. Tiny clumps of dry soil and crud crawled up my pants legs.

The sun blazed down from a blue sky, as clear and hard as a crystal dome. Its rays drew the thin dry air skyward in shimmery heat. It radiated from the glistening white faces of tortured rock, from the blinding, shifting white sands.

And that's when I heard the hissing rattle and saw the snake.

I tried to tame my racing heart by recalling that a rattler could only strike half its bodies length. I sloooowly moved back, almost stumbling over my own footprints in the sand, giving this evil creature plenty of extra space.

I discovered my dry lips weren't soothed by my swollen tongue. A harrowing thirst bit into me, as the wind kicked up, spreading out across the sandy wastes. Dust devils played here and there, little whirlwinds that sent spirals of sand spinning into my throat and eyes, raising a fog of choking grit.

I tied my handkerchief over my mouth and nose, bandit-like, and trudged on to nowhere.

Somewhere in the thick cloud of dust and sand, I heard an eerie sound, like hoof beats. Tack, tack, tack. When you were lost in the desert, you could take a single step in the wrong direction and be gone forever.

CHAPTER 9

Someone called my name with a question mark after it. Someone tugged and pulled at my right shoulder, causing it to painfully pop.

I turned my head in supreme pain and strained my neck to find the glaring flame of the sun and a shadowy silhouette sculpted above me.

"Here," Wayne drawled, "drink slowly."

I thought it was another mirage until I tasted the muddy liquid pouring down inside of my parched throat.

Wayne drew his revolver and capped off a round that impacted the earth inches from my left ear.

I jumped up, screaming, "Jesus!"

"No," Wayne drawled. "Scorpion."

There was a high-pitched ringing in my head, as I inspected the divot next to a pile of rocks where the evil insect had once lived. My legs wobbled and the world tilted.

"He'll be all right, but you better get that salve on him before he starts to blister."

Hands picked me up as if I were a child, and I didn't care who saw it. All my pride had been blown away in the sandstorm. I saw the angelic face of Rosita as she nursed my scorched face and neck.

I crawled slowly into the back of the jeep. Slate slumped there beside me, still unconscious, but breathing.

I gasped out a sentence from a bad movie. "How'd y—you—g—get here?"

"We followed the most likely trail of a fool." Wayne seemed to think that was funny. "You're damn lucky that this little lady told me where to look for you."

There was an abrupt lurch forward as the jeep surged up an incline.

I took a deep breath and found that my time in the desert had cleared my sinuses and burned away my cold.

❧❦❧

"Coffee?" Rosita handed me a cup and three aspirin.

By evening that day, we four were back in Brackettville. I'd been tended by the medical staff on the movie's payroll, feeling battered and baked like a plucked chicken.

I'd survive, they said, but I'd have a hell of a sun and wind burn.

I sat up in a creaking army cot and held the paper cup of warm brew with both hands. Those little paper handles never worked right. My lips were chapped and bleeding slightly, my head still ringing faintly, my throat parched like sandpaper, my eyelids inflamed. I was beat to hell, but it could have been worse. I could have been a dead beat, sort of.

John Wayne's voice rumbled from deep in his chest. "You're still not all here, are you?"

The nurse rearranged the white streak in my hair. "He's all right, but he's lucky we don't have to pull bone out of his brain. I prayed for him."

Oh, yeah—my head hurt too, something fierce. But I didn't want to show it. The coffee scorched my lips and tasted of Chap Stick. But I tried not to show that either. "When the going gets tough, I sometimes imagine I'm in a movie."

Wayne leveled his eyes at me. "Well, get up, Mr. private eye." He set his own cup on a storage crate marked *sombreros and serapes*. "Your movie's over, and it's time to go home."

A thought struck me. "You two know each other?"

Wayne raised an eyebrow. "You could say that we've met."

Another thought. One more and I'd be another Einstein. "Where's Slate?"

Rosita leaned over and stroked my forehead, explaining that the medical team had put Slate in another room where he couldn't hurt himself. They had him restrained to a bed, because he appeared to keep reliving the worst moments of our time in Mexico over and over.

I said that I wanted to see the tough guy as soon as I could get up and he was awake and alert.

"He's tough, all right," Duke answered. "His grandfather was a buffalo soldier."

"What's that?"

"Black Seminoles, originally from Florida. They were army scouts at the end of the last century, disbanded right before the First World War. Lot of them around this part of Texas, especially near Fort Clark. Like I said, tough."

Rosita took back my half-empty paper cup. "I'm afraid that Slate may not recover. We still do not know what was injected into his blood stream, or how toxic it is. But, right now, his biggest fear is that he cannot see."

"The stuff they pumped into him made him blind?"

"No—and *si.*" She gazed down, looking her most angelic. "He lost his contact lenses."

"He—he wears contacts?"

Wayne nodded. "Probably didn't want to undercut his hard-ass image."

That was about all my battered brain could take for the moment. I slid back down onto the cot and slept for a few more hours.

സ

I awoke famished and found that I'd been smelling breakfast in my sleep. They'd brought in steak, eggs, toast, coffee, juice, and a mound of hash-brown potatoes. I ate it all, like a wild dog. Then, probably out of revenge, the kitchen sent me a slice of rhubarb pie, and I called it quits.

I tested my legs and found that I could move about upright, like some dull-witted thing that had crawled out of an ancient sea, except I found that my socks and shoes where full of enough sand to build a castle.

I also found a bathroom and showered there for a full ten minutes, trying absorb moisture and wash away Mexican turf from deep in my ears and nose.

When I looked in the steamy mirror, I saw that portions of my face appeared patched together with partly cooked bacon. My skin was so tender that I decided to wear my chin stubble proudly like a pioneer.

Now that I was up and about, I learned that we were all staying at the ranch of James "Happy" Shanen, the mayor of Brackettville and the man who'd convinced Wayne to build the fake Alamo and film it on his flat and barren site. Shanen was a pudgy-cheeked man with big, dark-rimmed glasses. He had brown hair, a mustache, and a wide smile.

My happy host came into my room, along with Wayne, Richard Widmark, who was starring in the movie, and the grim and dead-eyed Sheriff John Sheedy. They all wanted to know about Dr. Zachariah Cortina.

Soon my throat became irritatingly raw again from telling my story over and over. I asked for, and got, plenty of cough drops.

They told me their story repeatedly, as well.

Wayne had gotten directions from the drunk in the cantina and, with the Mexican authorities, had arrived at the clinic early in the morning. The Chinese women there had been bundled off to a hospital in Piedras Negras, where they were being treated for mental problems similar to those of Chet Smith. Wayne had flashed some American green and the constabulary of Ciudad Acuna promised to shut down Zachariah's medical facility for good.

Dr. Z, his bodyguard and the "microbes" were not to be found, but Rosita showed up and lead the Duke to where Slate had been left to die in the desert. With her help, Wayne had searched for hours, finally tracking me six miles from the site where the remains of several other bodies were later found.

I wondered if the Mexican authorities would be able to do anything about the situation. They might even quietly be sympathetic of Dr. Z's theory and methods. After all, he'd said he owned them.

The local police on our side of the border weren't much help either. "We can do very little about things that happen in another country, even when we have hard evidence." Sheriff Sheedy looked intently at me. "Which we don't."

I felt my temperature rise. "My face is the evidence. Look at what they did to me."

"Maybe they pumped happy juice into you, like they did to Slate. You could have imagined the rest and wandered off for forty days and nights, boy."

I came to my feet. "Listen, Sheriff—"

Wayne raised both his hands in mock surrender. "Now, calm down, the both of you. What is that stuff, anyway?"

Rosita's voice came from the entranceway. "It's a psychoactive hallucinogenic. Zachariah called it Silver Snow because its lysergic acid came from fungus grown on grain stored in played-out silver mines. He mixed it with two other psychotropic ingredients, peyote cactus and a strain of wild mushrooms."

"Well, whatever it is," the sheriff groused, "it's what caused Smith to kill the LeJean woman. He's confessed to the crime and the two men who were with him that night confirm that he did the deed."

"Then, you don't need me," Wayne said.

Sheedy hiked his thumbs into his broad belt and sighed. "I think the judge will still want you to testify, Mr. Wayne."

"Christ on a stick," Duke complained. "I don't have time for this." He turned to our host. "Happy, can't you do anything about this? You're the mayor, for God's sake."

Shanen backed away without a word.

Wayne tried to appeal to the sheriff again. "I have to get back to the set. We're shooting a key scene with Linda Crystal tomorrow."

Widmark leaned in to leer. "It's a love scene."

Duke didn't look at him. "Shut up."

The sheriff shook his head. "I'll see if I can arrange for a closed session or for you to testify in writing."

Wayne smiled. "I'd appreciate it. We're already two weeks behind schedule. Costs are mounting up. I'll even need Pappy to shoot some exterior actions scenes."

My throat was still dry as toast, but I looked around at the group standing there. "Where is Ford, anyway?"

Rosita answered. "In his room. He is very sick in the lungs."

That didn't sound good, but I wondered about something else. "And, where is Dr. Z?"

"Who the hell knows," Wayne shouted. "Forget him."

Under the circumstances, I quickly replied, "That'll be the day."

Later, after things quieted down, I found time and energy to roll myself in a wheelchair down a gleaming tiled floor to the Firewrangler's room.

He was awake, looking better than I felt.

I wheeled over to his bed. "Hey, four eyes."

His face slumped. "Ah, shit."

"Yeah, I've discovered you're Achilles Heel."

"So, is my jaw supposed to drop, Kimo?"

I laughed. "I think it already has."

He froze. His eyes stared ahead, possibly seeing what the movies call a "flashback."

"Hey, Slate. You still there?"

He lifted his unbandaged hand, trying to snatch at something. "Rainbow, blood flowers." Then his face turned fierce and he bared his teeth like an animal.

This did not look good, especially when he began to yell and twist his neck and head as if to escape. "Get it off. It burns. Burning me!" the Firewrangler cried out in a guttural voice.

I yelled too. "Nurse! Get a doctor in here, fast!"

There was a rush of footfalls and a lot of scurrying around by the medical staff. I got pushed aside, while they stuck him with a needle full of something, waited for something, and finally told me to give a holler if something else happened. The wonders of medical science.

I rolled my chair across the windowless room to settle next to his bedside.

Maybe it was because he looked so beat up, or maybe it was because of his scarred dark skin, but Slate suddenly reminded me of Max, the FBI agent who'd been blown up last month by a bomb meant for me.

"Okay, Buffalo Soldier. Rest easy." I patted his inert,

rock-hard forearm. "I'm on the case and will see it through to the end."

CHAPTER 10

At times, I still felt as brittle as uncooked spaghetti and, other times, as limp as a slice of cheese. But my mind seemed intent on food, so my body must be on the mend.

While recovering my strength, I took a short time off to read the newspaper. My home town LA Rams had beaten the Chicago Bears twenty-eight to twenty-one in the second win of the new season. George Marshall, World War II general, former Secretary of State, and Nobel Peace Prize winner had died at age seventy-eight. A B-52 bomber carrying two nuclear weapons had collided with KC-135 over Kentucky. No radiation was reported.

Over in the comics, Kerry Drake was working on a kidnapping, Simon Templar was in Geneva tracking

smugglers, and Steve Roper was investigating a protection racket with Mike Nomad. None of them were getting
beaten up, burned up, or hopped up. Guess that was why
they were called the funny pages.

Then a small story at the bottom of page six caught
my attention. There had been a rash of drug-related kill-
ings involving Chinese in San Francisco. Nothing too un-
usual for that part of the nation, but it goosed the hair on
the back of my neck.

 espen

It was time for me to report back to Ford in payment
for his retainer.

His room was a mess. Clothes and books were piled
everywhere. Next to his bed was a copy of *Gods, Graves,
and Scholars*. The night table was littered with pencils,
paper, a glass of amber liquid, an ashtray piled high with
the black remains from his pipe, and a wadded, greenish
handkerchief.

The old director sat under the covers, on top of five
or six pillows, and in light green pajamas, still battling a
bout with pneumonia, but he still insisted on smoking his
pipe. He got up when I came in and moved to a low in a
chair with high arms, almost a throne. He seemed upset
with life in general and me in particular.

I'd been yelled at by the best, but he set a new stand-
ard for swear words per sentence.

I stood my ground while his pipe went out and he dug at the bowl with a pronged tool, dumped the dottle onto the floor, and unrolled a leather pouch that he'd taken from his back pocket to thumb in more of his intoxicating shag. I reached out my courtesy lighter.

He stared up with one gleaming baleful eye and grudgingly drew in the flame. "That's enough of that." He puffed for a moment and then coughed deep in his chest. When he recovered his breath, he said, "You're not much of a snooper are you?

I rose from my chair and leaned on a low chest of drawers just to stretch my stiff back. "Maybe not, but what happened to me in Mexico proves that Wayne wasn't involved in the murder. And that's what you wanted when you hired me, soo…"

He thought about it. "A man you can't kid is a man you can't trust."

Ford had just completed filming on *Sgt. Rutledge*, a story about the Negroes place in conquering in the West. "Maybe my next movie should be about the Indians' terrible past."

We sat together and discussed race relations—Hispanic, Chinese, Negro, Indian. "You'll find that race is at the heart of almost every human endeavor. Doesn't matter if you're Irish, Spanish, African, or Asian. People are suspicious and withholding of each other, and most times don't even know it. It's ingrained in their skin—and just as shallow."

The old man made some good points. I was quietly inspired to think that I, and maybe all of America, was unconsciously prejudiced, but I didn't see any way out of it. We'd been that way for too long, and it would take a lot longer for us to change.

I would have liked to talk more with him. I had a few trivial questions about the making of his film, *Stagecoach* and its "Hiya, Buck" line of dialogue. He still didn't look all that well to me, but I figured I'd earned the right to ask at least one film fan question. "What's your favorite movie?"

At first, I didn't think he was going answer. Then he winked. "Anything by Sean Finny."

⌀⌀⌀

I walked slowly down the corridor toward the spacious living room.

The hallway was long and narrow, with whitewashed walls, Spanish pictures and hangings, and Navajo rugs scattered over the red tiled floor. The living room was about the same, except wider with rough exposed ceiling beams radiating out to the far walls and dark heavy wooden furniture and pretty lamps with tinted glass shades. A full wet bar occupied one side of the room, extending under hunting trophies and beside pictures of local ball teams and barbershop quartets. There was a modern console TV stereo, as big as a Cadillac, parked along the other wall in front of an L-shaped sofa. I eased into a big leather chair beside the cold fireplace and let myself sink down.

Rosita entered from an opposite hall with a tray containing cups of coffee and dainty cakes, hardly larger than silver dollars. She had changed into a ruffled long dress with orange, flowering spots and a neckline that ran horizontal, exposing her broad, yet delicate shoulders.

I glanced uneasily out through the big-screened doorway behind us and got up without a word to go outside. The dark-blue desert night, peppered with stars, stared blankly back at me. Far off, I could see the flickering lights of the film set. Something was always going on there, day or night. They had a schedule to keep.

The evening twilight filled the Cinemascope veranda with the scent of sagebrush and fertile grazing land. I listened to the muted chords of soft western voices coming from somewhere like the ghosts of the Sons of the Pioneers. I later learned that our host, Happy Shanen, imagined himself quite the singer. He even spoke of a desire to someday cut a record of slow cowpoke tunes.

A shooting star streaked across the night sky and a whiff of wind flicked the half-dozen candles set randomly around on the low furniture of the flagstone terrace that overlooked the empty pasture and the runway of a private airport.

I took a deep breath, half wishing for a cigarette, and stretched my legs out in a cushioned lawn chair beside the gurgling swimming pool. Wayne and Ford and a few other principle members of the cast and crew were back inside somewhere drinking, rehearsing, and making changes to the script, no doubt. Occasionally, I could hear a shouted argument or a ripple of laughter.

Then I heard a swishing sound and turned to find that my Mexican nurse had slid open the screen and followed me out, as if wanting to ask or tell me something.

"You'll need a shawl or wrap, if you intend to stay out here for long," I said.

She gazed up at the stars, and I saw the underside of her chin and long neck. Some parts of west Texas were almost beautiful.

"Enjoying the evening?" Her voice seemed hopeful.

"I'm sorry. I don't think I ever caught your full name. I think you already know mine."

Her dark eyes became friendly. She made the slightest of curtsies. "I am Rosita Fey De Silva." Fancy name and she pronounced her first one like "Rrothita."

"I don't believe I ever heard about your relationship with Dr. Z, either."

"Dr. Z?" Her brow tightened for a second. "Oh, *comprende*." She seated herself in a padded chair next to me and wiped a strand of midnight hair from her eyes. "We were dirt poor when I grew up. I was the youngest of the four children who lived. I had two older brothers and an older sister, Carmelita, whom I adored. She would have fought a pack of wolves to protect me."

The accented tones of her voice charmed me—almost hypnotized me in my weakened state.

"I still remember how defiantly Carmelita's eyes bore into the sweating face of the last man who tried to dominate me. She hissed like a snake and growled like a wild cat, striking back with her claws and sharp teeth. I saw the man laugh and slam the back of her head. I tried to stop him, but he carried her away. When my brothers returned from gathering our neighbor's stray calves, they followed after her. Jose never came back. Manual returned wounded. It was the first time I had to be a nurse.

"But there were only two jobs I could take to earn a living. One was as a cook in the landowner's big house like this one." She moved a small open palm toward the lighted room and building beyond. "The other position that I could assume was also in his house, but I didn't like it. I worked hard in the kitchen for almost two weeks before I was forced into the other position—you understand?"

I felt a stab of sympathy and nodded.

"Manual hobbled throughout the stable, tending the horses and repairing the leatherwork, while I—I stayed in the big house, day and night. I finally could take no more abuse and ran away, leaving my Manual behind." She sighed, looking out at the still water of the swimming pool. "I traveled on foot almost twenty miles to the next ranch. I stole a horse and rode it to near death before arriving at Nueva Rosita on the Arroyo de la Babia, where

Zachariah took me in to work at the St. Anthony clinic. I was safe at last. My long nightmare was over."

It struck me as I listened, how terrible it was, even in this day and age, to be born of low Mexican heritage. In fact, it was no heritage at all. It was hell. I could almost understand Dr. Z's motivations and actions—almost.

She sighed again and placed her hands, palms up, in her lap. "Except—except for what his bodyguard began doing to me. The rest, I think you know."

ↄ◌ↄ

I slept poorly that night—physically uncomfortable, mentally indecisive, restless in the truest sense.

In the morning, we all met back in the vast living room—Wayne was now wearing overly sweet after shave and a coonskin cap that ogled me.

The full story of Dr. Zachariah Cortina was as convoluted as a mystery, inside an enigma, wrapped in a tortilla shell. It was like a rattler that had swallowed the Gordian knot.

It didn't make sense that this pulp fiction plot to restore honor to Mexico and bring down part of the United States would benefit only a single individual. There were greater motivations behind it. There were land and property rights involved with this somehow.

It appeared that there was a large organization at work—not just one man with a warped idea and the drive to carry it out. Dr. Z's little abortion clinic and his infected Chinese women was too big an "operation" to be managed by a lone operative.

The disruption of *The Alamo* movie was symbolic. The real target of this viral attack was land and American real estate. And the weapon of choice seemed to be illegal Chinese aliens, or even undocumented immigrants—regardless of race. Almost a second Civil War.

Wayne wondered about Z's methods. "Why Chinese?"

"Probably, he didn't want people from his own country to be carriers of infection. Traditionally, other nationalities and races have found the soft under belly of the USA to be the best point of illegal entry."

"It was simply a convenience, *Padrone*," Rosita offered, "a group of people easily at hand for his purposes."

I wondered if this could be a clue to Dr. Z's current location.

Rosita was another enigma. At least, to me.

I was surprised at how I felt about her. She had nursed me back to health and was now leading me to the man I was tracking. She didn't need to help me. She could have stayed in Texas. Something was driving her to follow Dr. Z. Something she refused to discuss.

I was fully aware that her actions could be designed to lead me into a trap. I felt as if her dark eyes never left me. And her hands had a way of finding mine, as well as other parts of my body, regardless of the circumstances.

She enjoyed speaking softly into my ear and took pains to touch the corners of my collar and shirt cuffs.

I'd met my share of *femme fatals*, but Rosita's allure had no purpose, except to attract me and pull me to her desires. Dr. Z didn't need her to bring me to him. He didn't likely know I was still alive, even. It was the other way around. She needed to be brought to Dr. Z, and I was pointed at the same target, so off we traveled together.

Maybe it was all a "snow job," but I felt that the attraction between us was genuine. And that bothered me as well, because it betrayed Suzi more than it put my own hide in danger. There was something mysterious about Rosita—something I didn't understand but would try to figure out. She was another mystery that I was determined to solve.

I told Wayne, Shanen, and Joe, who'd come to check up on me, about the newspaper article I'd read regarding the Chinese deaths in San Francisco.

Wayne's eyebrows went up. "I've a hunch you're on to something, Mr. Detective. I'll pick up your fee from where Pappy left off."

"Plus expenses?"

He'd been in the business a long time and was ready for that one. "Plus expenses."

Rosita confirmed that the good Dr. Z and his bodyguard might have rushed off to San Francisco. While I was naturally thankful for her information, I couldn't help suspecting that she was up to something. I made a mental note to check deeper into her background the first chance I got.

When lucid, Slate agreed that he'd heard Dr. Z mention the Chinese in San Francisco.

Despite all that had happened, we had no solid proof that it was Dr. Z who had drugged Chester Smith at the time of the murder. Neither Rosita's testimony nor mine would amount to much in the case. Wayne had his attorneys working on getting evidence imported from the Mexican authorities, but that would take time.

What was important was to find Z as soon as possible and try and bring him back. Then, we might have a chance at exposing the truth about the stabbing death and maybe the plot to infect the country with the silent snow virus.

"You're a detective, Wade. It's up to you." He didn't say "pilgrim," but I heard it just the same.

By now Z and Guy, wherever they were, must think that Slate and I were dead.

Wayne offered me the use of his private airplane to travel to Frisco. Rosita needed to come along to help me locate the Doctor there.

Up until now, I'd been satisfied following Slate's lead, Wayne's demands and Ford's requests… and what had it gotten? I'd been beaten and nearly killed. Slate had been infected and near death. All on account of this nutball doctor who had a vendetta against "White men."

I decided that it had to stop. With Rosita's help, I'd

find the crazy drug doctor and execute my on prescription for vendetta. She may not be 100% trustworthy, but I wasn't going to let that stop me from stopping him. Besides, I would be unique—the only private eye who travelled with his personal nurse.

Before I left, I shook hands with Wayne and Ford and apologized to Joe for losing his hat.

"That's all right, Stan. You've done enough cowboying. Get along now, doggie."

Rosita and I climbed aboard Wayne's plane, a Cessna Apache 310, just like the one in the *Sky King* television show. The engines buzzed as we elevated into the sky. I looked down from the side window and saw a black shape circling the Alamo movie set below on Happy's expansive ranch. I knew it couldn't be the same condor I'd seen in Mexico, but I still whispered, "*Vaya con Dios*" and eased back into the cushioned seat.

After we leveled off and the co-pilot came back to check on us, I gratefully ordered a Pepsi.

PART II
BRAINSTORM

CHAPTER 11

Sunday, October 18, 1959:

This time, I was the one who slept through the majority of the flight. At least, I tried to, but Rosita kept nudging me and my mind kept pestering me. Earlier in the day, she had dabbed makeup from a compact and tried to make the skin around my twin shiners match the color of my cheeks and forehead. Now she was doing what she called "guapo touch-ups," but I had the feeling it was just another way she could assure herself by touching me. It wasn't only my face that she liked to be in contact with, but also the backs of my hands. I must have had "the skin she loved to touch." Ah, the intrepid and tough life of the jet set.

Meanwhile, back at the ranch I called my brain, a corral-full of high-spirited thoughts trotted and paced back and forth, bucking to find a way over the railing of recent events.

Was Doctor Zachariah really what he appeared to be? In some respects, his actions were like something out of an old *Batman* comic book. It was a nutty reference on my part, but his underlying motives did remind me of a foreign evil genius who wanted to destroy our country. At least, that's what I thought he'd professed. Yeah, sure. Maybe I'd been doped up at the time. Hard to remember now.

More likely, he was just another nutcase, which meant he was a lot less predictable than a comic book villain and a lot more dangerous. It would be a challenge to locate him in San Francisco, especially since I didn't know my way around that big "City by the Bay." I wondered where I could get a guide that I could trust and not put into danger.

Assuming that Dr. Z was indeed in 'Frisco, how would I find him? Was he for certain connected to the murder cases there that I'd read about? Who were the dead female victims? Why would anything like that be happening—a series of murders, almost like something out of the movie serials?

I didn't feel that I had enough evidence on the killer to take to the police for follow-up. At least, not yet. Again, I had very little to go on, and it would be an uphill battle, trying to locate Z—unless Rosita knew something.

And what about Rosita? She sat there across the aisle from me on the plane, quietly filing her nails. Despite her having helped Wayne save Slate and me from death in the dry desert, I wasn't sure deep down that I could trust her. She seemed sincere with her, 'I'll help you, if you help me," but even with her soft eyes and warm smile, I couldn't get myself to fully buy her story.

Maybe I was losing my boyish optimism, becoming at last hard-boiled and cynical. Except, I couldn't figure that she had anything to gain by lying to me now. And she did, in fact, act as if she were attracted to me—as I had to admit I was beginning to be to her. I decided finally there wasn't much I could do about the Rosita situation right now, so I might as well sit back and enjoy the ride.

After our plane landed and re-fueled first at Roswell, New Mexico, and then again at Flagstaff, Arizona, we arrived at last in the late afternoon at Oakland airport on the east side of the Bay. Thunderstorms forced us to circle the field as the fuselage shook and I aged ten years through a long, shuddering descent.

Eventually, we bounced down and I exhaled. A few minutes later, I was still wobbling when I stopped at the Avis counter and rented a red, four-door 1959 Pontiac Bonneville. Wayne had loaded me up with enough cash that I could afford a little luxury for once, so I thought, Why not?

We drove up Hegenberger Blvd and across the Bay Bridge in the heavy downpour, while the radio announced that some Texan, named Johnson, had declared he'd be running for President. I recalled that Suzi's family was from SF and considered looking them up, time and weather permitting.

The car's windshield wipers batted overtime and the engine sputtered a little in the heavy shower. I figured it might be a vapor lock in the carburetor and feared we'd need to get it checked or fiddled with.

Following Route 40/50, transferring from one bridge to another over an island in the middle of the bay, we finally exited the James Lick Skyway to navigate the city proper. Within minutes, I found that this jigsaw town is hell to drive in.

First there were all the crazy streets, broken off at forty-five degree angles, probably the remnants of the 1906 earthquake. Then there were all the hills—up and down—hard to see what was coming at you until you reached each crest. Then there was the fog blocking and hazing your view until you needed your high-beam headlights just to keep from crashing into the normal auto traffic and the abnormal cable car traffic. Sheesh! I should have taken a taxi, instead of a rental.

Even though the rain was letting up, at one point, from on high near Mason and California, I saw slugs of fog oozing in, like creatures from an Allied Artists monster movie. Enormous fuzzy white caterpillars edged down the streets between the buildings, silently absorbing sight and sound. I had to remind myself that it wasn't stop-motion animation, as I fought down an almost overwhelming urge to run for my life.

Concentrating back on the streets before me, I told Rosita, "The fleet must be in."

She rested a hand on my knee. "Why do you say that?"

I gestured with my chin at the sailors in blues all over the sidewalks, jumping on and off cable cars, and generally clogging the downtown district.

"Oh," she said. "America, the strong."

I parked the Bonneville on the street outside the St. Martin apartments, a three-story, red-brick building next to a taller hotel. I never saw so many fire-escapes in my life—again, probably the result of that quake fifty-three years earlier. A spider web of power and phone lines ran from pole to pole above the street, intersected by a bramble of TV aerials and antennas on every roof.

We stepped around a clot of tourists with home-movie cameras, standing absolutely still as if they were afraid any movement on their part might blur the camera's image.

Still operating on Wayne's wad of cash, we checked into rooms at the Taylor Arms on O'Farrell Street. The place sported a six-story light-blue façade with bay windows and a tall red neon sign over an arched entrance and green awning. We passed a few tenants, and I decided that my hotel neighbors who worked in and visited this haphazard town were an intricate mixture of races, colors, and creeds. Just like it said in the US Constitution.

Riding a buzzing elevator up to our rooms on the fifth floor, Rosita touched my arm. *"Perdoneme, Padrone,* I do not wish to sleep alone."

I'd sort of anticipated that, so after installing her in room 510, I went back down and canceled the reservation for room 512.

It was as if the elderly Asian desk clerk had been expecting me. He scribbled a note in his ledger, took back a key, handed me a twenty-dollar refund for the first night's lodging, and smiled with the yellowest set of dentures this side of the Pacific. I even got a wink, which made me think about sharing one of my black eyes with him. But I remained a good *guapo,* or *guano* American. I couldn't afford any more trouble.

Back upstairs, Nurse Rosita and I shared a room-service dinner of cheeseburgers and watched the small, rolling television screen. Edward R. Murrow interviewed some hairy, toothy senator named Kennedy and Jack Benny's guest was, surprisingly, President Harry Truman.

Rosita took a shower, while I thought really, really hard about our relationship. She came out one time, long dark hair still dripping, wearing a skimpy white towel, and I almost fell out of my chair.

I knew I wanted her. And I was damn certain that she

wanted me. But there was Suzi to think about. And I thought about her a lot—my mouth getting drier and drier. I called room service and ordered a couple of bottles of Pepsi. Rosita came out again, brushing her hair and wearing a soft flowing slip and bra. My collar felt tight, so I loosened it. She came over to help.

There was mirth in her eyes. "Can't you trust me a little? If I hadn't believed you could save me, I would have run away instead of staying with you."

My hands naturally went to her hips, while her fingers stroked my neck.

"You are so strong and resourceful. Help me, Mr. Wade."

Her lips parted and there was a knock at the door.

We drank our Pepsis and switched off the TV. I told her I'd decided to pull two of the cushioned chairs together and sleep there, while she took the bed. My nurse frowned, then smiled, then slipped under the covers, sighing slowly and pulling the chain on the nightstand lamp.

Maybe I'd been concussed, after all. Or maybe I blacked out from being hit on the head too many times, but at least, that night, I didn't dream of clowns.

When I woke up the next morning, I found myself still fully clothed, lying on the floor with my back threatening to kill me if I got up. Rosita had already risen and ordered us breakfast. It was the room service knock on the door that had brought me back to consciousness.

We munched toast, sipped hot coffee, and watched

some dumb game show and a rerun of *My Little Marge* with Gale Storm, while planning our assault on the Golden Gate City.

I phoned my contact at the FBI. Again, without any hard evidence, there wasn't much they could do, but they'd get back to me. Then, I rang up my number-one client and "handler," Walt, but his secretary said he was out of town attending the funeral of George C. Marshall. I struck out a third time with a call to Sam Ellery, a CIA operative and part-time Elvis impersonator that I'd met during an earlier case. But he was on assignment with some agent named Oswald who was entering Moscow, Russia. So, for the moment, it looked like Rosita and I were on our own.

She stood at the window, where the rain had lessened to a gray mist. "What do we do?"

"I don't know about you," I said, tying my shoelaces and slipping into my shoulder holster and coat, "but I want to know more about that lysergic acid stuff and those murders."

Her eyebrows tightened slightly. "And how does a detective do that, *por favor*?"

I checked to be sure I had the room key and took her hand as we went out the door. "By visiting the best source of information in the entire nation: Ye Ole Public Library."

Getting directions to same from the desk clerk, who also wanted money up front for the long-distance phone call I'd made to Disney Studios, Rosita and I discovered that the sun had actually come out to shine on the recently drenched city streets. Knowing that we were probably taking our lives in our hands, we decided to walk the six blocks south and west to the center of the city and the main library on Fulton, in the Civic Center across from City Hall.

On the way down Larkin Street, we passed a second-hand clothing store. Again using Wayne's money, we each bought a trench coat. Rosita found a yellow whaler's cap and several of those clear, accordion-folded, disposable rain bonnets. I passed on wearing the funny yellow hat and took up a fedora, instead. It would get soggy, but I'd look cool in it as we continued our journey through moist San Francisco.

The library was one of those Carnegie buildings I'd seen in several cities—a massive block of steel and concrete three stories high with arched entranceways, and no stone lions. Inside the main reading room with its high beamed ceiling, globed chandlers, and tic-tac-toed windows, we sat at a broad, varnished table and read newspaper accounts of the recent homicides and missing persons, especially those who were female and Chinese. All of the accounts appeared in the interior of the papers— never the front pages. It was as if the publishers and editors didn't want to alarm their reading public.

Rosita took time to locate a few fat medical volumes containing recent research on lysergic acid and its various forms and uses. A team of doctors and psychiatrists at Berkley were analyzing the substance's "mind-expanding" properties. We located one article that confirmed Dr. Z's statement of military research being conducted at The Battelle Institute in Ohio. Under a subheading entitled, *Upsets Behavior Patterns*, I read that LSD-25 had weirder effects than nerve gas. An army general hinted at a new kind of warfare, without guns or bombs. A "psycho-chemical" weapon, of which "less than a pound would cause all the inhabitants in New York City to take on a schizoid reaction, i.e., an emotional disturbance marked by such things as delusions and hallucinations." General Creasy went onto say, "In six hours, with the opposition temporarily and harmlessly reduced to so many babbling idiots, enemy invaders could march in without firing a shot."

I wanted to know more, of course, especially since Rosita said that Dr. Z's version of this stuff had been combined with two other mind-bending drugs from cactus buttons and mushrooms. No wonder the resulting drug had been powerful enough to put down a man as strong as the Firewrangler. God only knew if he'd ever get up again.

I couldn't bring myself to imagine a thousand victims like him—crazed, in pain, and delusional.

We went back to the librarian at the reference desk, hoping she could help us dig deeper. She looked at us through cat's-eye glasses and said that the other journals we wanted were currently being read by "that gentleman over there."

She tugged on a double row of pearls at her throat and indicated a man seated at a far wooden table under the high vaulted ceiling, leafing through the pages of the *San Francisco Chronicle* and making notes in a small notebook like the one I carried. He had the highest forehead I'd ever seen and a scruffy brown beard, turning to gray.

Rosita and I thanked the librarian and casually went back to our chairs. We waited quietly there until around four o'clock when the man finished his jottings, rose, zipped up his wind-breaker, and headed for the exit.

CHAPTER 12

The man with the high forehead left through a side door of the library, and we dashed after him. Light drizzle kissed our faces as we followed him up Market Street. I could see, in the faces of the sidewalk crowd, the same desperation I'd noticed earlier in the expressions and postures of the people at the rodeo in San Antonio. I wondered if it showed on me as well.

We could have doubled back to the car, but that would take far too long, so I decided to try and use a clever tail.

We worked our way about a half block in front of Forehead Man. Rosita was confused and anxious. "Why are we not following behind? Certainly, we will lose him up here ahead of him."

"Not necessarily," I told her. "I've got a secret weapon."

A few months back, I'd had a tooth knocked out and, while at the dentist, I'd picked up one of those mouth mirrors. Later, I'd broken off the handle, keeping the little round mirror in my pocket with my spare change. I palmed the reflective surface now, raising it to the side of my head, as if rubbing my temple, and watched that the guy from the library, a half block back behind us.

We continued past the triangular buildings on Market, stopping and letting High Forehead pass us just as we reached the cable car rotating at the intersection in front of Woolworth's to head back up Powell Street. I couldn't resist laying a hand on the image of a Pepsi bottle cap and helping push the trolley around. Our man boarded the car. We grabbed hold of the tram and came aboard from the back entrance.

I shouldered my way quickly coming up behind High Forehead and whispering, "My name is Wade. Stan Wade."

He shifted around, worry in his eyes. "No, it's not. He's a fictional PI from *The Maltese Falcon*. Hammett."

Having heard this sort of thing about my name before, but never in 'Frisco, I tugged at my earlobe. "I'll keep dat in mind, pal."

He swallowed and then wagged a finger at me. "Ah, no, you don't. That's bad Bogart."

I sighed. "Okay, I'll start over. My name's Wade, not Spade. But you're right; I'm a detective."

"Sure. And I'm the son of a sea cook."

The cable car's bell clanged and people hopped off and others jumped on as we grumbled to a stop.

I got a business card out of my wallet. Sand dribbled onto the floor.

He took the card and then handed it back as the car started up again. "Anyone can have those printed." He glanced at Rosita and then up above my eyes. "Or wear a fedora."

"I give up. Just answer me one question. Why were you researching LSD at the library?"

He had an odd smell about him that I couldn't place. It was familiar and enticing. "I'm a writer. Perhaps you've heard of me."

Rosita chimed in. "Research on lysergic acid and the military? Research on dead yellow women?"

"I'm Philip K. Dick. I do a lot of research for my novels. Mostly science fiction."

A bell in my head rang, matching the one on the cable car. It couldn't be. This guy was my pal Norman's favorite author.

Rain began pouring down again. And my stomach growled.

I looked out as we passed Geary Street and pointed to a restaurant. "Let's get off this merry-go-round and talk where it's more private, before we all melt."

⌘

The dimly-lighted place was paneled and ceilinged with California redwood and called Lefty O'Doul's. According to the menu, this bar and grill was based on and owned by an ex-left-fielder and baseball coach. The walls were lined with framed photos of ballplayers like Babe Ruth and Ty Cobb. From what I could gather, Lefty had played left field, naturally, for the Phillies in the early 1930s and coached the San Francisco Seals in the early 1950s. He was even credited with bringing America's favorite past-time to Japan.

We ordered from the list of traditional menu items: hot dogs, red dogs, and pups in a blanket. When they arrived along with our drinks, we discovered humorously that all of our orders were the same.

I sipped a Pepsi with ice, Rosita drank plain water, and Dick reached into the breast pocket of his sport coat to take out a couple of tea bags, which explained his odd smell. He dipped the bags into a mug of steaming water. Cheap, too.

Dick waved his wiener at me. "These are outstanding."

I couldn't resist responding with, "And, they are mild."

Rosita knew something was up, but she didn't know what. *"Donde hables ustedes?"*

"We're talking about baseball," Dick said, and the nurse seemed to accept his answer.

We huddled together for under an hour in this quaint little sports bar, comparing notes. At one point, I thought detected something burning back in the kitchen, but I was used to that, since my own office was in the rear of the Brown Derby. "So, why were you reading up on LSD at the library?"

Dick licked mustard from the side of his right thumb. "It's mind-boggling and causes an almost mystical experience. That kind of thing is important to my writing."

"Psychedelic," Rosita said over the background strains of "Take Me Out to the Ballgame." Her eyebrows rose. "Have you ever been under its influence?"

Dick came back with: "Are you kidding?"

I responded: "I don't know. Are we?"

"Reality is hard to define," he explained. "And it's as soft as tissue paper, sometimes."

I reached for more catsup. "So it's something like getting drunk on a maryjane reefer?"

"Yes, only a thousand times stronger."

I mimicked Jerry Lewis' old line, "Are you for real?"

"Exactly. That's the essential question." Dick seemed driven, almost possessed to tell tales. He said he'd recently taken to taping his thoughts and stories with a seven-inch reel-to-reel recorder. Then he'd pause just sitting there, thinking, casting his mind out somewhere, spinning new ideas and nightmares.

I didn't know how to take this guy. A harmless kook? A maniacal paranoid? A creative genius with a warped perspective? I settled on the title he'd given himself: a science fiction writer. And you had to be a little creative, paranoid, and kookie to try and be an author, right? Yeah, the same could be said for my chosen field.

"Imagine if you will," he urged, "a guy named Joe who discovers self-aware intelligences generated from the complexity of particle interactions. This puts him in a sort of superposition, which means that there are two of him. And one goes on trial for murder, while the other is at large, investigating, trying to prove he's innocent."

Maybe that burning smell wasn't something back in the kitchen. I sipped my soda pop. "I think I saw that in an episode of Superman once."

Dick put down a slice of pickle. "I don't just write SF, you know."

Rosita tilted her head. "A serious writer?"

"I just finished a mainstream novel a few months ago. It has almost nothing whatsoever to do with science fiction."

I munched another bite of my ballpark frank. "What's the title?"

"Confessions of a Crap Artist."

Maybe he was pulling my leg. "Does it have a wow finish?"

"No… more like Fitzgerald's dying fall."

"Let's get back to you and the LSD drug."

Rosita cleared her throat above the big band sounds of Joltin' Joe DiMaggio. "Do you believe that it is connected to the recent abductions?"

Dick stared at her, mouth slightly open.

I leaned in. "The murders, remember, of several Chinese women in the city?"

He arched his back. "Is that what you're investigating? I'll bet there's a good story in that, brother. Matter of fact, I did hear something about a free clinic over near Ashbury where the beat crowd go to de-tox."

I didn't quite get the connection, but any lead was better than no lead at all. "Can you take us there?"

"Well…" Dick seemed hesitant. I thought he was going to hit me up for a ten-spot. "I guess it *would* make a hell of a stigmata story—but are you sure I'll be safe?"

I got up, put my hat on, and paid the check. Triple play.

✄୬✄୬

We walked a couple of streets over, through the mist on glistening sidewalks, a wild wind plastered our coats to our backs and urged us down the hill. Dick held back as the rain let up, but the sky was still a concrete gray. Given a chance, I thought he might make a dash for it, so I got him between Rosita and me until we reached the Bonneville.

After we'd piled in, the writer directed us from the back seat. "The clinic is somewhere over near Golden Gate Park." He guided me through cross-town traffic, down Market Street to Haight, while we listened to Conway Twitty sing "It's Only Make Believe" on the car radio.

"I wasn't entirely honest with you," Dick said from behind me. "One of the abducted women was a friend of Anne's."

I steered the wheel while glimpsing Dick in the rearview mirror. "Who's Anne?"

"Oh, I thought I said. She's my wife. There's a little shop south of the panhandle where she sells her jewelry."

Rosita and I exchanged squints. We were probably both wondering what sort of woman would marry a loser-type like him. I shrugged and went back to driving, noting that he'd known one of the victims. No wonder he seemed a little fearful. It struck me that we were taking him to a place he didn't want to go.

We found the Hidden Treasures shop in the 1600 block of Oak. I parked and looked out at the green expanse of the city park where clusters of people of various colors and dress enjoyed the respite from the rain. One guy seemed to be reading poems to anyone who'd listen, and a young couple in matching T-shirts tossed a tiny flying saucer back and forth, nearly hitting the bearded poet's shaggy head. I was fascinated how the little disk seems to float, defying gravity.

Everyone appeared laidback and beatnik-y. I sidestepped a pothole, but couldn't completely avoid a shallow puddle. "Looks like the city's low-rent district to me."

Dick cleared his throat and spat, climbing out of the back seat. "Freeway ramp is supposed to come through here, so the property values have dropped."

I turned and stared up at the red and white TV tower rising in the distance. It must have been a thousand feet tall and a true eyesore, if there ever was one. Then I remembered my own sore eyes and kept my thoughts to myself.

An ice cream vendor peddled past, steering an oversized tricycle. Dick halted him and bought a Fudgesicle. "We need to check in here," he called, heading for the knick-knack shop.

We crossed the street in front of a series of staggered Victorian homes. The eye-popping dwellings had to be at least a hundred years old. They shouldered each other with their bay windows hanging out toward the park.

Hidden Treasures was two stories high. The shop occupied the bottom half of the building and the top half had to contain living quarters, I figured. The entrance was centered between two large display windows housing an assortment of relics and curios that would have made a pack rat drool. On the walk in front of the store hunched bins of used books and magazines that briefly attracted Dick's attention.

While we waited for him to finish licking the last of the chocolate from the wooden stick, a guy with a guitar and attached harmonica strolled past. Dick glanced up once at us, his hand resting on a stack of digest-size volumes. "I love to read *Fate Magazine*."

Rosita held her hair in place against a light breeze. "Can we go in now?"

Dick rolled his eyes to the right and left, as if he'd just arrived. "Yeah, sure." He gestured at the door.

I was the first to enter the shop. A tiny bell tinkled overhead. There was a lot of artwork, pottery, and general brick-a-brack throughout the place. A couple of glass cases contained cufflinks and arrowheads. A wooden bowl full of Indian-head pennies sat on a counter top next to a brass cash register. Stacks of books, both hard- and paper-back, sat on the wooden floor and leaned against each other, the walls, and a couple of looking glasses. The air smelled of jasmine or joss sticks, and my sinuses knew it immediately.

Behind the display counter stood a young, over-weight man of Rosita's height. He had a voluminous shock of brown hair that blended down to his equally brown and un-kept beard. On the bridge of his nose was a pince-nez attached on each end to a black ribbon that hung around his neck.

He'd smiled when we first entered, but then said, "We don't need any more pendants, Phil. Sorry."

I stepped around what appeared to be an elephant's foot containing a couple of used umbrellas. "We're looking for the free clinic. Can you direct us?"

He removed the pince-nez. "The air is free, man, and healthy for all to consume."

I picked up a magic eight-ball and looked at the bottom. "Ask again later."

Dick moved past me. "Oh, come off it, Al. Are you still looking for free love?"

I got out my wallet, displayed my PI credentials, and quickly flashed my Captain Midnight Secret Squadron membership card. I tucked my wallet away. "And you are…"

"Ginsberg. Allen Ginsberg." He glanced from Rosita to Dick, as if to avoid me altogether.

I drew his attention by tapping on the top of the glass case. "And you own this place, Mr. Ginsberg?"

"I work here—part-time. But I'm really a writer, like him." He nodded at Dick. "If this has to do with those dead girls, I've already told everything I know to the other pigs, uh, police detectives."

From the rear of the store, through a set of beaded curtains that tinkled softly as she rustled through, a slim Asian girl arrived. She wore a long straight dark blue dress; no jewelry; and round, black-rimmed glasses, like Mr. Moto.

Ginsberg stepped back to let her join our conversation. "This is Li Finn. She used to work at the clinic, but…uh…hangs here now. Li, these are part of the multiple million private-eyed monster."

The girl bowed slightly and went to sit on a piano stool beside an antique desk.

We all turned to her with interested looks. She picked up a deck of worn playing cards and began to shuffle them with slow chopping motions. "I can answer all your questions."

Now it was my turn to clear my throat. But I didn't spit. "First, tell us who you are."

She set the deck of cards down in front of her and stared at it. "I am lost. Afraid and lost."

Rosita moved nearer to me and entwined her fingers within my non-gun hand.

Li Finn wet her lips with a small tongue. "I came to this country in my mother's belly, seventeen years ago. I was born in an internment camp, during the war, though we were not Japanese."

Dick dug out his notepad and started writing in it. Ginsberg looked around and found a scrap of paper and pencil and did the same. *Writers are compulsive creatures.*

"My first memories are of the smell of bleach and steaming, soapy water. My family operated a laundry on Powell Street until just last year when it was destroyed by a fire set in a neighboring building. It was caused by a couple of hobos wanting to keep warm."

I could identify with her story, since my own office in the Faraday Building had burned to the ground only last year, causing me to eke out a living in the back of the Brown Derby.

"I lost my family in the fire and I was moved into social services housing with dozens of other children and teenagers. But I knew I couldn't stay there."

I wondered if Rosita found this tale sympathetic. The expression on her face was intent on the girl's features.

"I was inspired to run away when I read a book called *Huckleberry Finn*."

"Sooo—" I drew the syllable out. "—your real name is not Finn then, is it?"

Her dark eyes bore into mine through round lenses. "I will never tell it."

I heard scribbling behind me.

"Allow me to tell your fortune."

I turned back to see the girl holding out her hands for mine. There didn't seem to be any reason to resist. In fact, I was sort of taken by the situation.

She studied my palm. "You are an interesting man," she began, in a way that every sucker had probably heard since Eve first tempted Adam. "I see that you are one who saves the lives of two presidents."

I couldn't catch my eyebrows from elevating.

"Do me," said Dick, edging around me.

She looked at his hand for a moment and actually turned it over once, possibly searching for a tattoo. "You will be a very famous writer."

"That's swell!"

"After you're dead."

"Oh."

Ginsberg mumbled something that sounded like, "Thank God, I'm not God."

The bottom of the magic eight-ball now said, "It is decidedly so."

The girl fastened her gaze on Rosita.

The nurse repositioned her hands behind her back. "We are wasting time."

"Yeah," Ginsberg agreed. "I already told you about the clinic."

I turned back to him. "Did you?"

"I can take you to the free clinic, if you like," the Chinese girl offered. "However, I won't go in. It isn't far. Follow me." She came to her feet and caused the bell to tinkle as she went out the door.

I was torn. This all had a weird edge to it. On top of our fantasy writer and the nurse, I wasn't sure who or what I could trust. I looked around the cluttered shop for a moment, hoping to find a map or maybe a compass. Finally, I made up my mind to go for it. "All right, let's go."

"Where?" Dick's forehead was wrinkled in confusion. I wondered about my own.

"After the girl—before she gets too far ahead."

Ginsberg's whiny voice followed us out the door. "Stay hip to the jive, man."

Moving around the book bins, I saw that the girl was almost a block away. Apparently, we wouldn't need the car in order to keep up with her. Then all that changed as she walked past a white Rambler station wagon. She was almost at the corner, when a man came around the front of the car, slapped her, and shoved her into the back seat.

I caught the sound of her stifled scream as I dashed forward, but I couldn't catch the wagon as it sped away.

But I'd seen the man before back when he'd been pressing a chloroformed rag in my face.

I tightened my hat on my head. "It's Guy. We've got to get him."

As we hustled to our parked Bonneville, Dick hollered, "What guy?"

CHAPTER 13

I stepped on the gas and our car sped past the round-lenses glasses lying shattered on the sidewalk.

The white station wagon was several blocks ahead of us, but we could see the driver and his unwilling passenger through its wide clear windows. She was struggling with Dr. Z's bodyguard while their car skidded around a corner, but once we followed through the turn behind the Rambler, she was no longer in view.

"She's not in the car anymore," Dick shouted from over my shoulder.

"Or they've knocked her out," I called.

Rosita grasped the dashboard with both hands. "He's rendered her unconscious."

I scanned the sidewalk as it whizzed by. There was

no sign of the girl anywhere I could see. "She must have slid to the floor. That's not good."

We thundered down Ashbury and took a right on Waller to the park, past the police station and Kezar Stadium, where I'd heard that the 49ers played football. Then we streamed west on Lincoln Way. It was a long straight street, with a couple of entrances to the park on our right-hand side. On our left were plenty of cross avenues with numbers from Eight to Forty-Seven, but the Rambler stayed on a straight course, barreling directly west.

We caught up twice at red lights, but I couldn't get our Pontiac in front of their car. I drew alongside at a stop sign, as they sped off before I could block them. We got hollered at by pedestrians coming out of the park and honked at by cars that we almost hit. I pounded the steering wheel and cursed our quarry and life in general. Then the engine began to cough and sputter.

I pumped the gas pedal to try and bring the car back to full speed. "Come on, Nelly-bell."

We chugged to the western end of the park, skidding to the right, the engine catching and holding again, and headed up the Great Highway with the beach and ocean now to our left. We accelerated and began playing dodge 'em like twin chariots in *Ben-Hur*, until my eight-cylinder motor pulled us slightly in front of their weak Willy's Jeep's engine.

I yanked the wheel to my right as we passed, cutting

the Rambler off just beyond an amusement park. At least, I *thought* they were cut off. But the white station-wagon braked to a halt, screeching and leaving a low black cloud of tire smoke, followed by a huge puff of gray engine exhaust, as it started again to push around us and up an incline in the highway.

I gunned the Bonneville after them—rocky cliffs on our right and a sheer drop to the Pacific on our left. We came to the crest of the hill and a cluster of buildings, parked autos, and a couple of Greyhounds full of tourists.

I gained fractionally on the other car, nudging them to the side again, away from a bus, while Dick yelped something about wanting seatbelts. This time I rammed them with enough force to crumple their right fender with the left side of my front bumper.

Both cars rocked to a stop. Mine hissed.

I jumped out, prepared for a confrontation. Guy held Li Finn close, probably at gunpoint, and headed for a big building under a giant *Cliff House* sign. I didn't get that far, because the Rambler's driver stood me off with a switchblade.

"Rosita and I'll go for a cop," Dick yelled. He may have been smart enough to get books published, but he wasn't as brave as a sack of hammers.

The guy with the knife grinned at me. His eyes were as yellow as his teeth.

Knots inside me got real tight. I had my own knife— a utility thing from my days in the Boy Scouts—but it was a clumsy assembly of screwdrivers, files, and open-ers. I'd used it once before in a situation like this involv-ing Bing Crosby and had gotten cut in the head, resulting in a week in the hospital and a white streak in my hair.

But—I had my gun.

I really didn't want to have to use it.

A gathering crowd of on-lookers moved forward slightly and then drew back.

The man with the golden face lunged at me, slashing. I moved aside as he went by, fast but not far, with bal-anced steps. While he turned, I ripped off my trench coat and draped it over my left forearm. I planted my feet, spreading my arms wide, acting as if I might be giving up. It drew him in. Too far in.

He stopped brandishing the knife back and forth be-tween his hands and flashed four-inches of steel at my face.

I raised my left arm and caught the blade in the folds of my coat, whipping off my fedora, throwing it at his eyes. The knife came at me again, but I caught his wrist and twisted it back as far as Detroit. The blade was point-ed upward now and we both hissed our breaths until there was a cracking sound, faint but audible, followed by a scream that seemed to shake new rain from the clouds.

The crowd gasped, but held their ground, watching the driver writhe on the blacktop. I shook the coat from my arm and didn't bother looking for my hat. Beyond the gawkers, I saw Guy take the girl down an exterior flight of stone stairs that ran beside a place called, Sutro's.

Dimly, I remembered seeing this location during the end of an Eli Wallach movie, *The Lineup*. It was an oddball emporium or *Musee Mechanique* with…what? an ice-skating rink? That *had* to be wrong. But it didn't matter now. I knew I'd lose Guy, if I didn't hurry and take those steps down, two at a time.

There was a concrete walkway at the bottom of the stairs, like the one around Griffith Observatory, only wider. Beyond a row of coin-operated telescopes beckoned the ocean and the sound of sea lions clearing their throats. I leaned leeward into a strong gale and knew that the rain would begin again any second.

Farther down the walkway, I saw Guy and the girl go into the wide dark mouth of a sort of garage. When I got to the single-story building, I found that it wasn't a funhouse. Rather it was an equipment shed, decked out with enlarged photos of Swiss chalets and housing a giant wheel. The grinding assembly drove a tram out to a cliff along a track that stretched sixty feet above a series of tide pools.

The tram, itself, was like one of the downtown cable cars in size and construction. It had accordion bus doors on the side at both the front and the back. Guy was pushing the girl into the front door, as I hastily purchased a ticket from a grandma in a booth covered with fake, painted snow.

I made it to the rear door just as it was hissing closed

and the tram began to move forward along its suspension cable. There was a lurch as we rose, becoming airborne. And that's when I saw Guy standing outside the tram on the forward platform with the girl, smiling and waving me good-bye.

I said a word that several of my fellow passengers didn't like. One even threatened to wash my mouth out with soap, if I were younger.

I sat, morose, as the blocky car crept along its cable, twenty yards out from the side of the broken windows of the old Sutro building. We went along like that through the heavy rain at a blazing speed of under ten miles per hour, while the waves kicked up spray below and the seals barked and honked at us from the black rocks beyond the shore.

When we reached the fake waterfall at the far end of the line and started back, I was composed enough to look down at the view and began to experience vertigo. Guy had completely escaped me. I was right back at the beginning—no closer to finding the man who had crippled Firewrangler than when I'd arrived in soggy Frisco.

❩❧

An eon and a half later, I got back to the Bonneville. The downpour had ended again. The jerk with the cracked wrist was gone and so was the Rambler station-wagon with the crumpled fender. Too bad I hadn't thought to get the license number, but even if I had it, what good would it do me?

The crowd had dispersed, but Dick was there with a security cop and—surprise, the China doll, Li Finn. Dick said that Guy had gotten away in the white Rambler with Rosita. She had simply gotten into the car in the place of the Chinese woman. I wondered about that longer than it took for the guard to tell us to get the hell away from his facility, Point Lobos, and Land's End and never come back.

When we left, a chilling fog was beginning to roll in again. What a delightful city!

✺✺✺

I wanted to take Li Finn to the free clinic near Haight and Ashbury, but she wisely wouldn't hear of it. We dropped her off, instead, at the Hidden Treasures and drove back to the Taylor Arms on O'Farrell.

The storm kicked up yet again, a full-fledged howling, ripping blow, drumming hard on the Pontiac's hood and roof. The windshield wipers whapped and smeared each blurring sets of headlights that approached, then swished past us.

I asked Dick to repeat what had happened with Rosita, but when he did, I didn't learn anything new. I took him up to my hotel room, fully disgusted with myself. He seemed more depressed than I, probably because of the friend he'd lost earlier to the threat we were feeling help-less about now.

All in all, we both felt inside like the weather out-side. He told me a literary term for that kind of situation, but I wasn't paying much attention just then.

I sat in a threadbare winged chair, toying with a glass ashtray painted with the hotel's name. "Look. This has been an ordeal for you, but I want you to know that I ap-preciate you helping out."

He sat on the edge of the bed, studying the tops of his damp shoes.

"I mean," I went on, "you're my only solid contact with the specific layout and details of SF."

He picked up the Gideon Bible from the nightstand and leafed through the pages. "Science Fiction? My best stories usually involve racial tension and end with the main character doing something like hugging a black man. Then, since our society isn't ready to accept that sort of thing, it turns out to be a dream of a twin who is on drugs, conspiring to overthrow the government in an-other dimension where he discovers he's really a ghost of an alien."

I tried to follow all that and wanted desperately to ask, "He, who?" but instead said, "No, Phil, not science fiction. San Francisco. You know this town, and I don't." I tried to sound reasonable. "I could really use your help to find Rosita and the people who took her."

He put down the Bible and started flipping through

the pages of the phonebook. Apparently, writers can't keep their hands off books of any kind. "What if they took her to that free clinic near the Panhandle Park?" he asked.

"No. I don't see them going back there now that they know we're on their tail. They'd go to some other bigger safer place to—Holy mother of pearl!"

One of those brilliant detective ideas hit me. I got up, walked over, and took the phonebook from his hands.

He raised his head to watch. "What? Do you know where they japed?"

I ignored his weird question and thumbed through the thin, yellow pages. I stopped at the Ms and walked my fingers down a column of tiny type. "Ah, ha!"

Dick came up to see where I pointed.

"Here," I told him. "There's a Saint Anthony medical facility on Macalla Road. Where's that?"

He closed his eyes, concentrating with his hand on his forehead like a mind-reading act. "I—I think it's out on Yerba Buena." His eyes opened. "Why?"

"There was a clinic in Mexico call St. Anthony's and Dr. Zachariah had a thing about San Antonio, so—"

"So, you think this Saint Anthony medical facility is connected. Could be, since yerba buena is Spanish for good herb, like marijuana."

"Not reefers again. I'm not going that far in piecing this together. Where is this Yerba place?

Dick went over to the window. He pulled back the

curtain and yanked up the sash, pointing at the storm in the night. "Out there. In the Bay."

⋲つⲉつ

Once again, we were back in my Avis rental, driving through the rain, the engine still sputtering.

Dick was sitting up front now. "So you really are a PI, huh?"

"Yep."

"Hammett was a PI, before he was a writer. Turn here."

I turned left, like he'd indicated. "Yep. So I understand."

"He lived here in San Francisco for almost ten years before moving to LA. I might do that someday," he mused.

At a stop light as we travelled east, I scrubbed mist off the inside of the front window with my sleeve. "I heard he had TB."

Dick shrugged. "Yep. So I understand."

"That's the real mystery, isn't it?"

"What is?"

Risking the fact that we were beginning to sound like an episode of *Dragnet* or *Leave It to Beaver*, I said, "Why would a guy with TB chose to live in all this damn fog?"

Dick coughed mildly, sympathetically. "The answer to that is simple. He was a drunkard."

I took the 40/50 on-ramp up toward the wet Bay Bridge.

CHAPTER 14

Who is she, anyway?"

The rain continued to slam down us as I pulled the Pontiac off the looping ramp that landed us on a quiet street of mature trees and ornate lamp-posts, all dripping.

"Rosita? I'm not one-hundred percent sure, but we've got to try and locate her, help her."

"Rescue her?" Dick asked. "You sure about that?"

"A man's gotta do what—what's expected of him." I thought my reply was lame, but Dick wrote it down in his notebook, so I went on and related the highpoints of my time in Texas and Rosita's accounting of her brothers' fates, including her own destiny with Dr. Zachariah Cortina.

"Sounds intriguing," the writer allowed. "And a little over dramatic."

I concentrated on my driving, not believing that you could have such thick fog in the middle of a rain storm.

We coasted quietly, getting our bearings while the Bonneville coughed, staggered, and finally stalled out with a gasping wheezed that would have impressed Jack Benny's Maxwell.

I tried repeatedly to fire her up again. The starter whirred and the engine whined, but we sat there dead in the water, literally, with dimness all around.

I climbed reluctantly out and took two minutes to pop the hood, unscrew the air filter, and finger-diddle the carburetor's butterfly valve—but it was still no go.

A street sign below the haloed globe of a distant dribbling lamp told us we had bumbled our way to Macalla. I knew we had to go down that mean, slick street to find our destination.

"I'll wait here," Dick offered. "Keep an eye on the car."

I was already soaked from coaxing the carburetor, so I just opened the passenger door and drug him out by his coat collar.

"Hey! Lay off!"

"Come on, you chicken. We're sticking together." I shoved him perhaps a little too hard in front of me, as if I intended to shoot him on the spot.

The maneuver worked. He went jerkily and hesitantly along the wet street, like an electric sheep. We passed three broad lots with flagstone entrances to their shadowed driveways. I could make out the big numbers on the sides of mailboxes and soon came to the one we wanted.

A manicured lawn and winding strip of gleaming blacktop led us past a wooden sign with a brass plaque, identifying the low mansion as the Saint Anthony Medical Research Center.

I sloshed up to the *port cochere* where a couple of dormant ambulances were quietly parked. Dick slipped on the wet grass and went down with an unsettling, "Oof."

"All right?" I whispered.

"S'all right," hissed the man who'd had taken the fall.

Yeah, easy for you, I thought as we rounded an unkempt hedge under an acacia tree.

We arrived at the building's entrance with a decision to make—ring the doorbell or sneak around the side in the dark. Dick had another idea. "Let's go and come back in the morning."

His was the reasonable approach, but we were here now, and I was determined to find out if my hunch about Dr. Z and St. Anthony held as much water as my slobbering clothes.

We circled around the side of the large lot just as the rain began to let up. I saw for the first time that the place was Spanish-style stucco with a tiled roof that drained into a cement flow-way. The shrubs and few prickly rose bushes were weedy and needed pruning.

Stretching up to peer inside a high window, I got a view inside. It was a déjà vu. Another laboratory, only this one was—

"Get your hands up. Turn around."

Yep. Another nice mess, Stanley. I let some air out of my lungs, feeling chilled, rotating my stance in the damp mulch.

"I'll take that gun," commanded Guy Wong from behind an automatic with an ugly silencer. "Why, Mr. Wade. A surprise. How nice to see you again."

"I'm not really here with him now," Dick explained.

"Hand it over, fingertips on the grip."

Lightning flashed and all three of us crouched a little. I lost the moment to jump him and tried to make up for it with calm repartee as he took possession of my .38. "Nice to see you too, Mr…What was the name again?"

He tucked my gun in the back of his waist band. "Joe Lombard."

"I'm not really here now," Dick explained again, while thunder rumbled over us.

"Shut up, baldy. I used to be a PI like you," he said, sociably. "Got hit on the head too often and one day decided enough was enough."

"You're not going to hit *my* head again, are you?"

He motioned with his long black automatic. "Wouldn't think of it. Get moving and keep your hands up."

We tromped back to the front entrance way.

"I'm not really—"

"Open the damn door, stupid."

We passed into a reception area with a few low chairs and a sliding glass window that opened into a nurse's station. Somewhere beyond a TV was playing. The polished tile floor collected our drippings and re-flected back the overhead florescent lights.

"Keep going."

My shoes squeaked and squished as Lombard point-ed us down a hallway with plaques on each wall until we came to the open door of an office.

"You're a very resourceful man, Mr. Wade. I thought you were dead back in Mexico." The bodyguard eased his bulk carefully around us and entered the office. "Get in here and keep those hands high." He crossed around a large wooden desk to sit in an oversized oxblood leather chair. A silver and blue marlin with a curved fin was mounted on the wall behind his head.

"The police know that we're—"

"Don't start with that," he snapped.

"Well, they do," Dick added earnestly.

He ignored us. There was a stack of papers on a leather-trimmed blotter. He chose to straighten them with the business end of his gun. "You want to see the doctor, don't you?"

My arms were beginning to tingle from being raised. "I suppose so."

"Good, because he's standing right behind you."

I swiveled my head to see past my elevated shoulder.

"Who is this one?" Dr. Z gestured with an X-ray film at Dick.

The writer backed away and bumped into a floor lamp, causing the room to appear to wobble. Then he saw there was no way to get away. "I'm just," he gulped, "one of God's favored fools."

"No." Our Mexican MD smiled. "You're an investment in medical knowledge."

I didn't like the sound of that and said so. The Lombard "Guy" rose up behind the desk and so did his gun. "Nobody cares what you think any more, Wade."

No more mister, I noticed.

Lombard chuckled at the doctor. "Shall I wrap them up to go, or will you want to eat them here?"

"I'm not—" Dick was sweating so hard his forehead began to cascade over his brow. My own back and arm pits felt drenched, and not from the evening's rainfall.

We were directed by the elongated gunpoint past a kitchen where I saw Rosita and another Chinese woman cooking something on a stove. I caught the nurse's flashing expression of surprise when she saw me.

Then Dick and I were shown to a doorway that led into darkness. I knew that if we went down those basement stairs, we'd never come up again.

CHAPTER 15

Can I first have a glass of water?" Dick said.

"Get going," the big guy ordered.

I took a step down, wanting to reach for the handrails.

"No, wait," Dr. Z called from behind us. "I think we can administer the solution here, now, and observe the effects later as they come on."

I brought my foot back up and shifted my weight around to see that the doctor exchanging the X-ray film he'd been holding for a syringe that Rosita handed him. More déjà.

Lombard waited while Z picked up a glass full of greenish-yellow liquid in his free hand. He nodded to his bodyguard, and Lombard smiled, accepting a similar glass from the Chinese girl. The liquid was thick and appeared frothed or frosted.

Rosita's face suddenly expressed disgust. I pretended not to see the hand beside her hip, gesturing in a calming manner.

The two men looked at each other for a beat and then they both raised their glasses in a clinking toast and drained them.

Dr. Zachariah finished swallowing and informed me. "Carrot, banana, and avocado tonic. Stimulates the digestion."

Rosita's eyes flashed a warning and her head shook microscopically.

Lombard laughed loudly at our expense.

Dick licked his lips, but didn't ask for anything.

I hooked the toe of my shoe under the bottom rung of a kitchen chair. "Health nut, huh, Doc?" The piece furniture was heavy oak, and I regretfully didn't think I could flip it from where I stood. Besides, my hands were already prickly and starting to go to sleep.

Dick's arms were now almost at his sides again. Nobody cared much what the writer might do.

"Rosita is an excellent cook. In fact, she's the only one who has determined the exact specifications for my lysergic and peyote formula. That's why she's still with us." He raised the syringe and came at me with the needle. "Take off your coat and roll up your sleeve."

Lombard waved the silenced pistol. "Just stick him in the neck, Doctor."

Dick began again, his voice a little cracked. "I'm— I'm not here with—"

Both Z and the bodyguard turned to him: "Shut up!"

That was the best opening I was going to get. I kicked the chair, sending it skidding across the linoleum to jolt against Lombard's left side, and I swung my right elbow around to knock into Dr. Z's raised hand.

The syringe went over and over in the air, almost stabbing into the wooden counter next to the sink. The glass inside gave up a satisfying shattering sound.

Dick tried to make an end run around the bodyguard, but the automatic came down on the side of his head and he actually yelped "Ouch" before dropping to the deck like a sack of wet sand.

I punched Z in the gut and shoved him away. He flailed around, one of his arms striking the Chinese woman, while his body jostled Rosita at the stove.

I got two steps past them and reached where Dick had fallen, when Lombard leveled the dark barrel of the silencer inches from my bruised but no longer black eyes.

"Easy, Mr. Wade. Do you mind if I call you Mr. Wade?"

Doctor Z got to his feet and worked a kink out of his neck.

My mouth tasted of bitter iron. "Do you mind if I call you an asshole?"

He knew he had me. "Not at all, sir. We all have one." The gun never wavered.

Z rested himself in the chair that I'd kicked. "Just who are you, really, Mr. Wade? We left you out in the middle of nowhere and here you are showing up—"

Lombard finished the sentence. "Out of nowhere."

I began to suspect a Liberace-sort of relationship between these two men, which partly explained Rosita's lack of interest in them, but I wouldn't let myself believe that this quack and his stooge were going to dominate me, so I didn't answer their question.

"Very well. I'll tell you who you are, Mr. Wade. You're a young businessman, working out of the back of a restaurant. You live in a thirty-year-old boat that seldom goes out to sea. And you have not much money in the bank. No close relatives, younger or older, except maybe a mother out there somewhere, even you don't know where—"

"I get it, already. You've checked up on me. What's your point?"

"My point is that you're nothing, but you have potential. The kind that I can use. And I'm sure my organization would pay well for that potential—perhaps as much as $10,000—provided your potential was applied in the correct direction, for the right cause."

The bodyguard didn't seem to like that idea. "Hold on there a minute, Doctor."

Z stopped rubbing his neck and raised a hand for silence.

Everyone else seemed to be holding their breath.

I massaged the last of the numbness from my fingers. "Go on. You fascinate me. So the nurse here is the one you rely on to mix your deadly drug, eh?"

"She was about to demonstrate to me how I can aerosol the solution, so it can be carried by the fog to affect thousands throughout the city. Thousands of Whites and foreigners who took this land from my people."

"That's not good," Dick said.

"No. I told you," Rosita said. "It won't work with heavy moisture. The hydrogen atoms won't combine properly."

"That's not bad," Dick said.

"How about $20,000 and I keep my mouth shut?" I said. "Or how about $40,000 and my partner here and I just walk away and never come back?"

Dr. Z's smile widened beneath his frameless glasses. He snapped the fingers of his right hand. "Oh, forget it."

Rosita obeyed his wordless command and passed him another syringe.

Lombard came forward with his automatic at the ready.

Before I could move, the needle was in my neck and the plunger pushed the burning drug into my bloodstream.

☙❧

It didn't come at me all at once. I sat at gunpoint at the table while they injected the same foul substance into Dick's throat.

He knew it was coming, whereas I hadn't, and he fought like a whining wildcat—to no avail.

The first sign that something wasn't right was when a rattlesnake lifted its head from behind Dr. Z's left shoulder. I prayed it would strike him suddenly and fatally, but it coiled its body around the man's ear and silently slipped inside, tail vibrating.

I shook my head and pressed my fingertips where the needle had struck my neck. "Uh-oh." There was a dull throbbing behind my eyeballs, like those little hammers in the aspirin commercials.

I got up and found that my legs were rubbery. I held the kitchen counter top and discovered I was spooning coffee into a percolator and plugging it in. I wasn't sure if those were my hands, or someone else's.

Somewhere, in the next room, the Frankie Ortega Trio was playing a Latin-beat version of "Dancing in the Dark." That seemed incredibly funny to me. Everything was tickety-boo.

Dick was wearing my favorite fishing-rod tie clasp, but he didn't have a tie on. Molly Marie O'Dee started quoting the Bible at me, while Walt said, "I've always thought of you as the son I never had." I smelled burnt lamb chops and tasted bitter crab-apples at the back of my throat.

"Next to a heel, you'll always find a good soul," Molly cooed, her red hair clashing with her green eyes.

"Is that from the Bible?" Dick asked.

"No," she answered, "Tom McCann."

"He's a boothead," Dick countered. "Ain't got the brains God gave a boot. I'm not here with him."

Dr. Z lifted one of my eyelids and peeked inside. "There's our fall guy."

Dick started describing the first private eye agency on Mars. He came over and shook me, but I shoved him away.

"Hey, kids, what time is it?"

I think I was weeping when I answered. "Captain Kangaroo time."

Mr. P helped Dick lift me up by the shoulders, while I wondered if I'd turned off the percolator.

Comedian Harry Truman was speaking quietly with ex-President Benny Kubelsky. "We've got to have a fall guy."

Z and his boyfriend floated together out of the kitchen, but they left a Mexican bandito behind to guard us. He wore a wide sombrero and crossed bandolier belts.

Walt Disney, Errol Flynn, Ian Fleming, George Reeves, Ross Macdonald, and Duke Wayne were pallbearers carrying Raymond Chandler's casket. Ray was enjoying the ride, waving at the crowds in the Marineland grandstand where Roy Rogers yodeled non-stop for fifteen minutes. During those ululations, a middle-aged private investigator came up, shook my hand, said his name was Archer, and bragged about meeting Orson Welles back in 1937.

I saw my brother, Josh, in the crowd, but couldn't get to him. He rushed to join my mother and the two of them slowly faded into the thick fog.

The bandito guard told me to settle down or he'd shoot me, *amigo*.

Things began to fall apart. Fall of the House of Usher. Fall of the Roman Empire. The Rise and Fall of Legs Diamond.

Rosita helped me drink a cup of perfumed tea laced with what tasted like orange juice. "My, you're a hardy boy."

"I'll be a blue-nosed gopher," I told her.

Dick slapped me.

Suzi rubbed her cat, Phooey, under my nose and I sneezed violently.

"Listen to the tape," Rosita said. "It's on the tape."

My pal, Norman, insisted that I wake up and read new pages from his novel.

"Be sociable. Look smart. Drink light refreshing Pepsi."

Dick's drugged face elongated and sang out, "Stay young and fair and debonair."

The Chinese woman stabbed me with a needle and left it in. Then, she stabbed me again and I began to get annoyed. She kept doing this, leaving the straight pins sticking out of the skin on my face.

"You're taking the fall," Bogart said.

"The hell I am!" I told him.

Rosita kissed me behind the ear and I caught a heavy whiff of her "My Sin."

Joe Louis, Peter Lorre, and Eleanor Roosevelt want-

ed me to go to the Royal Hawaiian Restaurant in Honolu-
lu.

"Hold it a minute," I told them all. "I'm getting a little confused."

Rosita unclasped the necklace with the single black
pearl from around her throat. She toyed with it, wrapping
the thin chain around her left index finger, and approaching the guard.

Mike Shayne met Mike Hammer in New York City.

The guard eagerly yanked the chain that dangled
from Rosita's finger. It spun the pearl, uncoiling and pro-
pelling it forward out of her hand at a terrific speed.

A couple of X-15s flew over, followed by a Soviet
missile, and a guy in blue and red underwear.

The black pearl cracked the guard right between the
eyes. Dick stepped in and landed an upper cut full on the
man's jaw, sending him slumping down into a corner beside the Hotpoint refrigerator.

Rosita shuttled me down the basement steps. We
went beyond an ancient furnace and coal bin, through a
back door, and came out under the stars.

Nightfall. Rainfall. Deadfall.

I could taste the fog. Not pea soup. More like cold,
gray vichyssoise. "When you're lost in the fog," I explained, "you can take a single step in the wrong direction and be lost forever."

Dick slapped me again. "Keep your voice down."

Thunder rumbled as we got into one of the ambulances.

Dick thumped my chest with the back of his hand. "Stay down. I'm going to get a weapon."

I thought I had this all figured out, but now I wasn't so sure. For a moment, my teeth chattered involuntarily.

I sat there counting my fingers, until I heard the sharp crack of a gun report. Somewhere, out in the foggy darkness, another shot rang out.

Someone ran to the other ambulance and started it up. I tried to realign my thoughts, while picking needles out of my forehead and cheeks, but my mind went off topic.

Dick jumped into the driver's seat next to me and fired up the engine. We began to move through the cone of our headlights, while he argued with the Noir Man.

I let them sort it out and watched us whiz past a guy with a dandelion nimbus of snowy hair as he lifted the wing of a burnished steel car and climbed inside. When I turned around to look back, he was out of sight.

Tack, tack, tack.

"Let's get the hell out of here," I urged.

"He's headed for the bridge and he's not getting away!" Dick shouted back, handing me my .38. "Not on my watch!"

I didn't remember him being this demonstrative before and wondered what the Famous Writer had been smoking.

CHAPTER 16

He drove like a mad bat out of hell. We were going to catch the other ambulance or die trying. "Giddy-up, go," I hooted.

"Did you see that?" he hollered back. "I almost ran down that black-and-white clown riding a motorcycle."

I sat there, dumbly starring at him as he hit the siren, and we came along side of the other ambulance. "You—you could see the clown?"

"Hell, yes, I saw him. Is the circus in town or something?"

"Something," I replied meekly. I was beginning to feel like my old self—I thought. That's when I saw Felix the cat use an exclamation point as a baseball and hit a line drive out to left field to O'Doul.

I shook my head to try and clear it. Words floated up from the blackness: "Ask again later."

The wind-whipped rain continued to pelt the ambulance as we rocked past a street sign for Hillcrest Road. The emergency vehicle we were chasing skidded to the right where white lettering and an arrow indicated the entrance to Treasure Island, but then our vehicle nearly tilted over, steering suddenly to the left instead.

Dick hunched above the wheel and gear shift, peering through our misted windshield. "He must know about the navy base and dead end. He's headed back the other way, shamus. Hold on!"

I cranked down my window, realizing that no one had ever called me that before.

Our ambulance plowed through the pouring rain and followed left up South Gate Road, heading east to the Bay Bridge. Lightning flashed and wind buffeted when we came along side of the other medical unit a second time.

"Shoot!" Dick shouted. "Shoot him before he rams us!"

Through the thunder and spatter that blew through the window, I aimed the handgun at the driver in the vehicle speeding next to us.

"Let's not be so damn hasty," the woman I'd killed in Vegas said.

I pulled the trigger and felt the gun kick in my hand five times. Then it just clicked repeatedly, so I set it in my lap.

The other ambulance skidded and dropped behind us. Dick slammed on the breaks.

The rain had slackened a little. When I opened the door and got my feet planted, I saw we were beside a concrete abutment supporting the bridge that seemed to tower above all the way to the moon. On the other side of a tall chain-link fence, gigantic I-beams stretched out and over the dark waters of the bay.

Our old acquaintance, "Guy," or Joe Lombard, worked his way out of his driver's seat and tumbled onto the roadside. He looked seriously wounded, but he still had his gun. The sound of electricity carried on the wind.

Dick dashed forward.

The bodyguard fired from his awkward position on the ground. Dick dodged to his left and grabbed the radio aerial on Lombard's wrecked and still-hissing ambulance. The writer snapped off the antenna. With the deftness of Don Diego, he used it like a sword to whip the weapon from Lombard's hand, sending it skidding along the street into the darkness.

Water began collecting in my open mouth.

Eli Wallack walked past and told me to close it. Edmond O'Brian claimed that if I didn't, I'd be DOA.

When I looked back, both Lombard Jand Dick were on the opposite side of the chain-link fence.

"Well? What are you waiting for?" Jimmy Stewart insisted.

I started to climb after them.

I flipped my center of gravity over the fence, avoided snagging my pant legs on the top, and fell next to a pile of enormous rocks that shored up the abutment. Dick and his quarry were clambering above me, gaining a railing that lead higher along the bridge's dripping beams.

"Geronimo, kid," said a guy who sounded like Bogart and had his face all bandaged like the Mummy.

I had no idea how I came to be feeling a regular pattern of rivets as big as my fist.

The bridge vibrated with a regular pulse from the cars and trucks on the decks. I found Dick about ten feet in front of me on the south side of the bridge leaning along a chest-high railing. Lombard was moving along in front of us, trying to climb off a ten-inch ledge.

Various pipes and cables ran along the ledge, and a honeycomb of corroding steel and concrete felt cold in my palms. A lone fog horn sounded from far off in the direction of Oakland, or Berkley, or Brooklyn.

I had a sudden overwhelming desire to climb back down and go see Suzi.

Beneath my feet, the ocean tides tore at the bridge's base.

I was caught in a web of diagonal braces and ladders with X-shaped rungs zigzagging between the trusses. Like a tightrope walker, I saw Dick reach Lombard and the two men began to struggle.

"I'm. Really. Here. Now!" the Famous Writer shouted.

Holding both my balance and breath in the chilled air and creeping along like a human inch-worm, I neared their tussling forms. Somehow, Dick got behind me on the slick top of a poorly-painted beam. Lombard clutched at my wet arms.

I tried to move back, hugging a post while Dick navigated to the next diagonal cross-beam.

Lombard had hold of me and wouldn't let go. We were suddenly like brothers.

Nudged by a cross breeze, my balance shifted. The toe of my right foot found and caught on something.

I heaved and hoisted myself, trying to monkey away. And that's when I slipped, dropped, spun, grabbed, missed, tumbled, caught, and dangled desperately.

Lombard hung like sixteen tons from my right calf and left ankle. Below him, the night waters churned and beckoned under the wisps of fog. The air was so thick that sounds traveled through it like a medicine ball. My fingers began to cramp.

Dick tried to get me back onto the bridge proper, but I was beyond his reach. I saw him come slowly to his feet, almost waving. Then my grip gave out and I was falling like something in a bad dream, remembering Bogart's last word.

ᕮᔆᕮᔆ

For the briefest of moments, I was flying, with the

wind in my hair. My flight was straight and true—straight down and truly terrifying.

I rotated slightly and saw below me in the distance the hazy lights of a ferry churning its way outward to oblivion, or Oakland.

Then Lombard struck the water a half-second before I did and the world turned into a bone-chilling aquacade.

I'd gulped a lungful of air on the way down and pierced the surface of the dark waters feet first, right after the bodyguard's body—which was exactly what it did for me. Had I hit first, instead of him, the impact would have shattered my spine for sure and my own body would have been driven so deep into the bay that I'd never have come up in time to catch a breath.

As it was, I bounced off Lombard, who took the brunt of the fall, and plunged farther down into the inky, wet world of Davy Jones, bubbling and clutching at nothing solid.

In a panic, I kicked off something after all, swinging my arms out and up, grasping to fly underwater, leaping for life. I felt like a mountain climber, clutching at the side of a liquid cliff.

Everything was black and wet. Black and ice cold. Black and silent. No sound except a faint gurgle. No view, not even a cartoon cat or clown.

I yanked myself in the direction I prayed was up and pushed away, struggling not to scream.

Something went *whoosh* and my head was above the

surface. I hauled in a lungful of air and heard my ears pop before I sank down again to fight a second round against my watery opponent.

The surface opened up again from above and this time I stayed there, dog-paddling and howling like a new-born baby. A wave slapped me, driving a gallon of water up my nose, and I coughed until I thought my eyes would burst.

When my vision cleared, I located the colorful string of tiny lights that must have been the shoreline. Then, the fog took them from me.

Swiveling my head, I tried to catch some sign of Lombard, but he might as well have been all the way back in Texas for all I could tell.

I took in another deep breath and yelled, "Help!" in a liquidly voice.

A distant fog horn answered. Too distant.

My clothes and shoes weighed me down. My strength would be completely gone in less than a minute. I struggled and shouted, "Help!" again. It was all I could do, except sink.

Some idiot called back, "Hold on," and I wondered what I was supposed to hold on to.

Something bumped me. I prayed that it wasn't a shark.

It bumped me again, this time on the right shoulder, and then it pulled at me.

I rose an inch higher in the water, having been gaffed

on the end of a pole like a tuna. I grabbed the wooden shaft and yelled, "Help!" once more.

Dick tugged the pole and me on the end of it. "What do you think I'm trying to do?"

I spouted water like Orky or Corky at Marineland and swam for the word painted on the back of the boat: *STARFLEET*.

Dick grabbed my hair, almost pulling off my left ear. "Get in here."

"Ouch!"

Within seconds, I lay face up on the rocking deck, panting, and rubbing my injured head.

Humphrey Bogart leaned over me. "Welcome to the fight. This time I know our side will win."

CHAPTER 17

A bolt of brightness flashed across the sky, followed by an end-of-the-world crack of thunder. "That, I believe, is my line," Victor Lazlo said, and the two men walked off together across the water and into the night and fog.

I coughed up another pint of bay water while Dick gunned the little boat's engine and headed into land.

I honestly had no idea how Dick had commandeered the small craft and located me in the choppy water. Detective work can sometimes be very mysterious.

As we trawled toward shore, hungry waves threatened to capsize us. I imagined that they were clutching in a repeated attempt to sweep me over the side and draw me back into the watery depths. I shivered and heard my teeth chatter.

We tied up at a low pier and sloshed our way back to where the ambulances were crudely "parked." Through the dim light, we saw that a couple of what had to be sea police—who must have come from naval base on nearby Treasure Island—had taken charge of the scene.

"Their rifles are at the ready." Dick lurked behind a dripping bougainvillea bush. "They must think it's an invasion or attack from illegal aliens."

I concentrated on keeping my chattering down to the sound of a pneumatic street drill. Considering my physical and mental state, I wanted no part of the SPs.

"What are you two doing over there?" a voice asked behind us.

I froze, still hunched.

"Picking berries," Dick said. "Why?"

Lightning flared and I saw Bogart again.

"Are you okay?" He had a cigarette dangling from his lips and rain dribbled down the end of it. "Come over here into the light of this streetlamp, so I can getta good look at you."

Dick straightened. "We don't want any trouble here, pal," he said, sounding like Philip Marlowe.

But we followed directions until the three of us stood next to a two-tone Ford.

Bogart looked young to me now, as if he were only a smooth-faced kid. His shoulders and neck were impressively muscular. His cheeks were a little rounder than I recalled.

The drug was still messing with my mind. Dick's mouth appeared to be full of stainless steel teeth. I shuddered. "I gotta sit down a minute."

They conferred for a long time, while I rang water out of my sleeves and pant legs and watched it in fascination as it ran down the gutter.

Dick walked back, accompanied by an impressive roll of thunder. "Come on. He'll give us a ride back to the clinic. Says his name is Gores and he's a repo-man."

I looked up at the writer. "I don't want to go there."

His face was dark in the shadowed lamp light. Gregg Toland would have loved the scene. "We've got to be sure that those women are all right. You hearing me?" He hauled me to my feet, just like when he'd gaffed me into the boat. "And I want another crack at your insidious doctor."

Cold, wet, and exhausted, I heard myself say, "But I'm beat."

The drug had affected Dick in a strange and somewhat terrifying way. "You're beat? I'll beat you like a gong, if you don't get going."

While we drove, the writer rambled on about race relations and how the Japanese and Chinese would soon dominate the economy. He said that a war in south-east Asia would consume the nation, Arabs would attack New York City, and the president would be a black man.

Under the circumstances, he got no argument from either me or our driver, but I slowly eased away from him, settling into the far side of the car's back seat.

Finally, the gory guy dropped us back at the clinic. I think Dick threatened him to keep his mouth shut and his nose clean, before the man sped off in his repossessed Ford.

My shivering had lessened and I was feeling slightly normal as we went inside the building.

The electricity in the place kept going on and off like in a funhouse. I saw my reflection flash in a hallway mirror and thought for a second that it was the fishman from the Black Lagoon.

The lights continued to flicker, and it seemed it wouldn't be long before they failed completely. My gun was long gone, lost in all this craziness.

I found Dick in the kitchen with the Chinese woman. She was the only person still on site, but a lot of things were weird to me at the moment. She gave us each a glass of milk, followed by another of orange juice. She talked about "aroma-therapy" and a book I think she called the *I Chang*. I used a dish towel to get some of the water out of my ears, while Dick listened to her go on and on about *The Book of Changes*.

Feeling moderately better, I conducted a brief search of the premises, just like it says to in the *Crime-Stoppers Handbook* and confirmed that Doctor Z and Rosita were gone. But where? The Chinese girl didn't know, or wouldn't say.

I wandered back to what appeared to be Dr. Z's office, where I saw the results of their hasty exit. Desk drawers hung open. Stacks of medical journals laid fanned out haphazardly on the floor.

I sat down in the chair behind the desk. I had no clue where they could have gone, which meant that the drug was still out there and Dr. Z was still capable of using it on innocent people, again.

He could be anywhere now in San Francisco, or California, or even America.

I was never going to find anything in this mound of paper. Reports and file folders were scattered across the desktop and carpet. I lost my temper and banged a fist on the desk blotter, making more papers tumble to the floor. I'd like to think that I did it because of the drug's residual effects, but I wasn't entirely sure of that. I wasn't entirely sure of a lot of things.

An ornate grandfather clock stared at me from the other side of the dark room. Tack, tack, tack.

I rubbed my temples, trying to concentrate on something else, while the florescent lights continued to blink and buzz above me.

All right. It was clear that I'd encountered a new version of Philip K. Dick tonight. He had suddenly become forceful, bold and violent in nature. The effects of Dr. Z's "snow job" seemed to crank up its victim's irritability, almost to a blood lust.

I recalled how Chet Smith back in Texas had reached for a knife and killed the LaJean actress. After which, he'd claimed he couldn't remember his vicious act. And I'd seen how the drug had transformed Dick from a thoughtful author to an aggressive combatant.

The basic ingredient of the lysergic acid was supposed to make people lethargic, I thought, but Dr. Z's concoction had the opposite effect.

So why hadn't it worked on me? Or perhaps, it had. The pit of my stomach dropped when I thought that it was a possibility that maybe I'd attacked someone while under the drug—only now, like Chet and Dick, I couldn't remember a thing about the action, assuming that it had even happened. I felt frustration crawling up my spine, filling me with confusion.

Was there some dark crime lurking now in my recent past that would someday come to light or jump out at me? How could I fully trust myself now? Or in the future? Including my upcoming wedding to Suzi?

More than ever, I wanted to find and stop Dr. Z and Rosita.

I knew I couldn't fully trust her. She had always struck me as knowing far more than she should. Z had even stated that she'd formulated this terrible drug. Was she possibly the true force behind all this? Was she part of that larger organization that the doctor had mentioned?

What had she told me? "Listen to the tape." What tape?

My eyes search the cluttered office and located a seven-inch reel tape recorder on the credenza behind the desk. Dick said he used one to dictate story ideas and plots. I'd heard that physicians often transcribed case notes through the little microphone plugged into one of these units.

I switched the device on and watched the reels begin to rotate. Hissing static for several seconds. The tape was probably blank. The lights in the room flickered again and winked out.

I held my breath.

The lights came on and the reels began to circulate again, dragging the dark brown tape past a series of small wheels. I clicked the "Re-wind" button and watched the tape spin back a few feet. Then, I hit "Play".

Dr. Z's voice came out of the tiny speakers. "…minor setback combining the solution and making it airborne, but we'll proceed at the main lab where we can better control the temperature."

The reels continued to spin, but no sound come from the player. Then, I heard a few pops and crackles and Rosita's accented voice said, *"Padrone, por favor,"* followed by what sounded like a coded message, "Sea sore sell vermin appear am out."

I banged the recorder with the side of my hand. The electrical storm must have shorted something out inside its guts, because it began to smoke.

I quickly rewound the tape and played Rosita's message back once again. "Sea sore sell vermin appear am out." It was still a mystery.

The tape machine got hotter. I started looking for the wall plug, just as the first flickering flames rose up from where the tape scrolled past the tiny wheels. I garbed a sheaf of papers and patted the thing down, until I could unplug it.

The fire had gone out. A small cloud of white smoke rose to the ceiling. Rosita's message was gone and my impossible mission was at a dead end.

The lights blinked twice and went out. I groped my way back to the kitchen. By the wavering light of the blue flame from the gas stove, I found Dick and the Chinese woman. "I can't find any sign of Dr. Cortina or Rosita." I fixed my eyes on the woman. "Do you know where they've gone?"

She shook her head, but I didn't believe her.

I pulled her up to face me. "This is important."

"Please," Dick said. "No violence.'

"No violence? After everything you did in the last hour? You almost wreaked a car, beat up a guy, and threatened another—and me, too. And now you tell me, no violence?"

He looked at me with that big head of his. "What are you talking about? I didn't do anything like that. It's against my nature."

The Chinese woman replied calmly. "He doesn't re-member."

Words caught in my throat like day-old, dry toast. I coughed and paused, gathering myself, and came back with a sensible, intelligent response that any normal person would have said: "What the hell—"

Dick flinched. "I would *never* do anything like that," he insisted. "Perhaps you were abducted by a vast rational mind."

"He will be fine," the woman assured me handing him another glass of OJ. "This and milk will counter-act drug. The police will come soon. Thus, the doctor will not return and face them. You should leave, as well."

The writer got out his notebook and started writing. "I'm really here now." He looked at the girl. "I thought she was dead, but we'll be all right. You can go."

Anger took control of me, shaking and pushing and forcing me to turn my back and leave them, the room, and the building. I charged out into the end of the storm. I stomped down the driveway, down the street, down to my rental car and got in, slamming the door.

I sat there, fuming. The effects of the drug were still in me. My crazy visions had let go, but my anger still had a fierce hold. The threat to the Chinese women of San Francisco seemed to be over, but Dr. Z was still out there. And I wanted to find him so bad I could taste blood.

In a rage, I banged my forehead on the steering wheel.

The pain had a sudden calming effect. I would probably get my black eyes back, but Rosita's voice on the tape now made sense. "Sea sore sell vermin appear am out." The words were garbled before, but they flowed together clearly now. I had to go find a Cesar Silverman at Paramount Studios.

PART III
SNOWSTORM

CHAPTER 18

The plane tilted and seemed to stand on one wing as it came down over the city. We swooped above the heavy construction around the new Jetsons-style LA international airport terminal and continued to descend past the erection known as City Hall. When the ship leveled off, we were on our way down to the sunbaked strip of the Orange County airport.

The wheels touched with a squeal of protesting rubber, and the plane was on the ground. Within minutes, the air tasted of car exhaust and my sinuses began to tighten in recognition.

Before checking out of my hotel room in San Francisco, I'd received a phone message from my contact in the FBI. When I called him back, I learned they still had no location for Dr. Zachariah Cortina, but they were oddly interested in my writer-friend, Philip K. Dick.

I wondered why the FBI would be interested in a lowly science fiction writer and couldn't come up with a good answer, except that the entire trip had been bad and strange and violent. It struck me that I'd been overtaken by a strong desire to hate, causing me to fire that gun without compunction during that ambulance chase, back in 'Frisco. Now, driving over to my office at the Derby, I wondered what had caused me to throw caution to the wet wayward wind. I wasn't my usual cautious—some would say, chicken—self lately.

And now that I thought it through, I seemed to recall that I had been pushing and shoving Dick around up there on top of that bridge—which was how he'd gotten behind me. I'd blindly charged into danger, intent on getting my hands on Lombard's throat.

My palms began to sweat on the steering wheel of my Thunderbird, and it wasn't from the noonday heat.

This drug was dangerous. It incited the animal urge to fight, as if a higher part of the brain were dulled enough for a sort of stormy darkness to take over. Almost like Dr. Jekyll changing into Mr. Hyde. Such a scenario would be like red meat to a Hollywood script writer.

I was caught in my own personal horror movie. Or maybe it was the result of all the fluoride they were putting in the water and toothpaste these days. How should I know? I just knew that it made me mad.

∽∾∽∾

I was still trying to cope with my feelings, while putting some polish on my water-stained shoes, when Norman limped into my office at the back of the restaurant. "Someone's trying to kill me."

I spit the Blackjack gum I'd been chewing at the trash can beside my desk—and missed. "Okay, we'll get him."

My pal, a sort of beanpole with a flattop, scowled down at the moist dark wad. "It's a her. One of my new girlfriends."

My brow rose. "You have girlfriends?"

He pushed his glasses up with a thumb. "And what's so strange about that?"

I reached down and shuffled the stack of mail that had piled up under my door while I'd been on the road. "Look, Norm, I've got a lot going on right now."

"This is important."

I shook my head because I still had water in my right ear, even after the plane ride. He must have thought my motion was a sign of denial, so I quickly answered, "I'm sure it is."

"You owe me," his insistent voice gurgled.

Damn! He had me there. I did owe him, especially for that time last month when he shot electricity into a guy who was about to kill me. "All—all right." I returned his full gaze for the first time. "What is it again? And what do you want me to do, exactly?"

"Candy tried to kill me."

Water drained from my ear with a *goosh*. I could hear clearly now, but I couldn't believe *what* I was hearing. "You have a girlfriend named Candy?"

"Why do you keep asking me all these questions?"

I gave up buffing my shoes and shoved the gear into a desk drawer. "Because, dammit, that's how detectives get answers."

Norman Weirick was an acquired taste and a necessary evil, who "invented" things I could use during my investigations. He'd given me mini-wireless recorders and phone bugs, tracking devices, and the prototype of a portable TV. Some of the stuff actually worked for a few days. He was a conspiracy nut when it came to Communists and a lover of monster movies and science fiction tales. Most people who knew of him called him "Weirdo" Weirick.

He stood there now, clacking parts of a slide rule back and forth, while explaining that she didn't really try to kill him. She'd just kicked him in the shin for not kissing her and he'd fallen over a fire plug.

I hesitated to ask, but couldn't stop myself. "Kissing her? Who is she again?"

Outside my office door, I could see that the shift had changed at the BD. All the waitresses were lining up at the time clock.

"She's a chemical micro-biologist that I met while working on our Artie Shaw case." When not asking me to read his latest novel or movie script, Norm assisted me on various low-level investigations. I was going to have to reconsider that arrangement.

"Getting kicked by a girl is not attempted homicide, Norman."

"It is, when you almost get run down by one of those city trucks spraying DDT to kill off the mosquitoes."

"Get out of my office. Now."

He gulped and took a step back. "Don't you want to hear what I found out about the Shaw case?"

I came to my feet and raised my voice. "Out, or I'll throw you out."

He paused, easing out the door. "Why are you so mean?"

I picked up a beer stein full of pencils from my desk, intending to throw it, but making a scattered mess instead.

I ground my teeth, growled, and slammed the stein back down. When I looked up, Norman had vanished.

Everybody wanted a piece of me. They all expected me to do something for them. But I felt over-exposed. I was fed up and a little like Scott Fitzgerald's "crack up." It would be great to just cast off the moorings of my boat, sail out of the Del Rey swamp, and drift with the current up the side of Golden State, the nation, and even the continent, until I reached that new, clean, white state: Alaska. Then they'd never find me. I could fish and freeze and die in peace.

But I'd promised Suzi that I'd come see her when I got back into town, so…

I locked the office and shuffled through the city's smoggy haze and glare, back to my car. Dropping gingerly into the T-bird's hot seat, I tapped my fingers lightly on the scorching steering wheel. I waited for the air-conditioning to kick in.

Walt had bought this showboat for me, after my Kaiser had been blown up. Then the car had been stolen. A friend on the police force had tracked it down for me while I'd been out of the country last month. Now it was cool enough inside to take a deep breath, so I shifted the gear into Drive and set off for Suzi's apartment though the lovely traffic up La Brea and into the Hills.

The radio popped on when I started the engine, but I snapped it off. Like Garbo, I wanted to be alone. I drove north without slamming on the brakes, leaning on the horn, or hitting another happy motorist.

It being late in the afternoon, Suzi was home when I got to her place and she immediately put out her cat, Phooey, because I'm allergic to the monster.

We talked. She was opening up new offices for Sunset Investigations in the Taft Building on, of all places, Hollywood and Vine. She'd gotten the job from Jerry Lewis, and it looked like she would soon get additional big-name clients. She'd started hiring operatives to handle the increased work load. One young guy sounded like nothing but trouble to me.

She was all business. I didn't like it. I thought she couldn't afford the high rent at the Taft and told her so.

We sat in her living room with the TV playing a new Frank Sinatra Timex Show, but I didn't give it much attention. I thought again about the *Cervantes II* and how keen it would be to chuck it all and sail away.

Just as Bing Crosby and Dean Martin were beginning to join Sinatra in a chorus of "Together," Suzi said that she'd missed me and wanted to snuggle.

I felt strangely anxious about being near her and caught myself pacing from the living room to the kitchen—where she kept the knives.

Once in a rare moon, when I'm on a case, something hangs at the back of my mind, waiting to come forth and help me figure things out. This was not like that. No, this something was back there prowling in my hind brain like a hungry circus cat, but it wouldn't come out. The skin at the back of my hands itched.

Suzi offered to make a cup of some exotic tea she'd learned about in Kenpo class, but I wasn't interested. She could tell that something was wrong and hinted that I'd been with another woman.

I denied it, but she wouldn't quit. She came right back at me again.

I paused, thinking of Rosita, which was the wrong thing to do. I could see the tears forming in her eyes.

She turned to leave the room and then came back. "Well?"

"Well, what?" my mouth shouted.

Her palm came up as if to strike the left side of my face.

My hand came back and slapped her. Not once, but twice.

Behind us, Crosby, Martin, and Mitzi Gaynor sang, "High Hopes."

Suzi dropped to the carpet, more from shame than from pain.

And I clinched my fists at my sides until the nails bit into my palms.

The word, "Shit," echoed off the walls.

She was up in an instant, shoving and striking my chest, ordering me to get out.

A hot, white rage swallowed me. It was like television static or snow in my head. My hand reached out and grasped the telephone receiver from an end table. My mind screamed, demanding that I shut her up and slam it into her head.

I stopped.

She had gone down on her knees again and hadn't seen my movement or intent.

I put the heavy weapon back down where it belonged.

She sobbed, staring at the floor.

I bit my lip, but could hardly feel it.

I backed away. Then I backed away some more. Then I backed away out the apartment's front door.

Sinatra crooned, "It Was Just One of Those Things."

CHAPTER 19

Time stood still.

My alarm clock had run down. I stood below deck, winding the key on the back of the clock, listening to the ratcheting clicks as I turned my wrist, and wondered if I should switch on another light. It could get deadly dark down here in the hold of my ship at night, but I figured that was pretty much what I earned and deserved.

I checked the glowing face of my brother's watch and set the clock for a quarter past midnight. I decided not to set the alarm.

The boat caught a slight ground-swell, shifting the deck beneath me enough that I had to change the position of my feet to avoid falling over.

Yeah, I deserved that, too. And a whole lot more besides.

I eased down onto my bunk, hearing occasional bells ringing out above deck and felling confused. My head started pounding again.

What had I done to Suzi?

What upset me more than anything else were those moments when I wasn't sure I was all there. The residual effects of the drug overtook me, and I became certain that something was wrong, but I couldn't tell what. It frustrated me to feel as if someone else were trespassing on my mind and controlling parts of my actions.

At least, that's what I wanted to believe. It wasn't me doing it. Was it?

I stood up and climbed the ladder to come out topside on deck under the stars and the three-quarter moon far up in the night sky over the black ocean. A weak breeze kissed my face, cooling the damp skin below my eyes.

I wanted to get back to the way things used to be. Back to where all I had to worry about was finding a job and getting paid. Now, all I was finding were feelings and impressions that I didn't want.

When I was growing up, my parents used to tell me, "Count to ten, when you get angry." That technique had worked pretty well, actually. The pause that refreshes— just like drinking a Pepsi. I remembered hearing that jingle: "Stay young and fair and debonair." I'd heard it in

San Francisco while I was under the full influence of that damned drug. Fu Manchu had nothing on Dr. Z.

I took a deep ragged breath and shuddered, as if to shake myself awake or free.

I was better than this. I helped people. I solved mysteries. I—I shot a woman dead in Vegas.

Tack, tack, tack.

"What the hell is that sound anyway?" I shouted into the night.

"Keep it down over there," a male voice from the boat moored behind mine cried back.

A faint mist rose around the *Cervantes II*. Far off shore, a steamer hooted long and low. Looking up at the stars, I felt incredibly small, puny, and insignificant. The black water seemed inspiring and inviting.

If I hadn't shot her, she would have shot me.

But did I have to kill her? Couldn't I have tried to at least just wound her?

A large sea bird, possibly a pelican, swooped past my head like an enormous bat and then vanished into the gloom.

She'd been driven by insanity and revenge. The cancer had eaten into parts of her brain. And the mob had killed her FBI partner. If I hadn't stopped her—dead—she would have set off that bomb, causing the deaths of hundreds of innocent people.

Part of me said that I did the just and right thing in shooting her. And part of me said it was all wrong.

Standing there next to the rail, separated from infinity, I realized at last what was making me so angry and mad. I'd been forced to be the bad guy, while needing to prove that I was the good guy. In order to save hundreds of lives, I'd been required to take a single life.

Mr. P had never had to kill—that I knew of. It had fallen to me to step over that line onto fresh, deadly soil. I was now one of the new breed of PIs who struck and shot women. I now lived in a noir world where things were no longer simply black and white. Things were gray and formless, like the fog or a sandstorm.

The source of my anger wasn't physical pain. It was mental stress and that damn drug.

It hit me then that I'd thought myself in a wide circle. Damn. Only one thing could break the cycle. "I stopped smoking. I stopped drinking. And I can stop this, too," I told the night. "And, I can find and stop and kill Dr. Z."

And then, I recognized that with the thought of killing, I'd gone full circle again. The violence was still in me—and so was the damn drug.

I crawled below deck, into my bunk, into a dark damn void.

❧❦❧

The deep growl of a motorcycle engine out on the pier nudged me from a heavy slumber. A guttural voice near my head rousted me further. "Good morning, squirrel. We brung ya breakfast."

The *Cervantes II* was a 1948 Taylor Cabin Cruiser, thirty-six feet long with an eleven-foot beam. Alexis Iglesia had helped me overhaul the engines back in the spring. She had been one of Mr. P's operatives before he'd retired, swore like a longshoreman, and had nursed my boat when it almost capsized. Now she was trying to nurse me.

Lex wore worn jeans and gray sweatshirt with "Vic Tanny's Gym" printed across her wide chest. "Ya look like road kill, sleeping ugly." She tossed the opinion over her right shoulder while she fired up my hotplate, preparing to grill a heap of bacon and eggs.

My old pal, Norman, climbed down into the cramped hold to join us. "Hi, boss." He still wore the same clothes I'd seen him in yesterday—blue and white checked long-sleeved shirt and brown slacks. He pulled a loaf of Wonder Bread from a Von's grocery bag.

I groaned slightly and watched while he squinted around the tiny galley.

"You need a toaster, Mr. Wade."

"Had one. Broke it."

My pal began clattering together the metal parts of my coffee pot, so it would brew properly. "Hey, Mr. Wade, I've got a new song challenge for you." He liked to tease me to identify old show-tune lyrics. "Ready?"

I yawned and stretched, resigned to the fate they'd conspired to force upon me. "Ready."

Norm's alto voice sang out, "'I don't know where we're going, but I'll stick to you like glue.'"

I headed for the head. "It's from the *Road to Utopia*."

Lex flipped fried eggs over uneasy. "You two are certifiable."

As I squeezed past, Norm pushed his glasses back into place at the top of his long nose. "So what's the next line?"

My stomach rolled over from the strong cooking smells. "Put'er there, pal. Put'er there." I closed the little door on my boat's toilet.

"Correct-a-mondo!"

I surprised myself by vomiting in the crapper.

Slowly, as my vision cleared, I saw a drawn face with a white streak of hair reflected back in the rippling surface of the head's water. It stuck out its tongue. "Hello, smart guy," we said. "Where's your brain today?"

I finished my business, spat a few times, and stepped back into the cabin, just as Lex handed me a plate of half-burnt eggs with a side of sizzling strips. I burped loudly, but accepted it.

"You know that beach-house of Lawford's, where I live?" she asked, "The one over his garage?"

I forked an egg and watched the yellow ooze toward the bacon. "Yeah?"

The fifty-year-old woman waved a spatula at me. "Well, I think he's banging Marylyn Monroe there."

I munched. "So?"

"So, he's not the only one. You know the Democratic Senator, Kennedy?"

"Yeah?"

She cracked her knuckles. "He's doin' her too, I think."

The eggs tasted delicious. "So?"

Lex had recovered from a recent throat cancer operation, leaving her raucous voice even gruffer when she laughed, "So, shit fire and save matches."

Norm poured and spilled a little coffee into one of my chipped Coast Guard cups and handed it to me. "I'm thinking about buying a gun."

I swallowed, somewhat audibly. "I guess that would be all right. What kind?"

Norman nibbled a slice of bread. "A machine gun."

"I guess that would *not* be all right."

Then, the Kid Who Reads Comics hit me with the loaded question: "When are you and Suzi getting married?"

I made as if a tiny chunk of bacon got caught in my throat. "Circumstances have conspired—to delay the ceremony—until—"

"What circumstances, Mr. Wade?"

I sipped hot coffee. "I don't know, Norm. Sometimes a woman wants to…wait a while before—"

"Oh, come off it, Squirrel. We know you guys had a big fight. Norman talked to Suzi about you and then he called me. Why do you think we're here? Huh? For your health?"

That didn't sound right.

"Actually," Norm corrected the woman, who had started coughing from her long speech, "we *are* here for his health. He might need therapy or something."

I noticed for the first time that Lex was wearing a wig. Her cancer chemo-treatments must have been taking a toll on her. "All right, gang. You win. The truth is that I've got this anger problem I have to figure out how to manage."

"Is it an addiction?" Norm asked. "Cause my girl, Candy, might be able to give you something for it."

"I've already got more than enough for it, thank you!" I snapped at him.

Lex put her plate down. "Maybe ya got a might too much, Squirrel."

"Yeah, we came here to help you, Mr. Wade. 'Cause, we owe you. You know?"

I felt the muscles at the sides of my mouth turn up. "Okay, here's the deal…"

Within minutes, I'd given them the whole story. The duststorm in Texas. The brainstorm in 'Frisco. The fight, the anger, the madness from the damned drug. It felt good to get it out, to spill my guts, to take a load off my mind. Slowly, it dawned on me that that's what good friends were for.

I finished up by describing the dark night and the far-off stars.

Lex listened and nodded. "When I look up at the night and see the twinklin' stars—" she grumbled, wiggling her thick fingers at the cosmos, "—I think how puny they are and how big I am. Grrr."

I had to smile at that. The old girl was still a tower of strength for me.

"Wait a sec!" Norm held his glasses tightly to the side of his head, as if it were going to explode. "You met—I mean, you actually met Philip K. Dick? He's my favorite—"

"I know, I know."

"What's he like? Did he give you any ideas about the future?"

"Sort of."

"What's he writing now? Something with an alternate reality?"

"I'll tell you later, Norm."

"Did ya get his autograph?" Lex said.

"No! He's not a movie star." I calmed myself. "All I know is that now, more than ever, I want to find and stop that Dr. Z. Okay?"

Lex's serious, topaz-brown eyes locked on mine. "Are ya sure you're up for it? Why not call the cops and let them handle it?"

I heard myself sigh. It took a while. "I've been beaten, drugged, shot at, and left to die in the desert, so I've earned this. And I just told you a minute ago that I made a promise to that Firewrangler guy. So, yeah, I'm up for it. Besides, it might be good therapy and make me feel right with the world again."

"Yeah," Norman said. "Why should the cops have all the fun?"

My coffee had gotten cold. "But I'll likely still need some help from my friends. You know?"

"That's the spirit." Norman laughed and snapped his fingers in a gesture of approval. "Danger is no stranger to me, cha, cha, cha."

"Sometimes I just wanna slap that kid." Lex's voice seemed to gargle.

Norm ignored her comment. "What's out first move?"

"I need to find a guy named Caesar Silverman at Paramount. And I need a new gun."

"Hey, hey," Norman cried. "I can help you with both of those."

Lex and I exchanged baffled looks. Neither of us believed his statement.

"Go on, hot shot, 'splain us dat."

CHAPTER 20

Lex headed out on her thunder bike and Norm and rode off out in my Thunderbird. The sky was clear and the smog light, for once. The guy on the boat behind the *Cervantes II* shook a fist at us as we were leaving. I think it was Roger Moore, who was working over at Warners on *The Alaskans* TV series.

Norman had been assisting Suzi with her Jerry Lewis case, and Lewis had just signed a huge contract with Paramount Studios, because the executives there were in a panic now that DeMille had died. I still read the trades.

The upshot was that Norm could get us into Paramount. In fact, he'd been working there with a friend in the prop department, refining a few of his so-called "clever inventions," such as a semi-bulletproof vest.

I paused at a stop sign so a ten-year-old with a flagged pole could let his classmates cross the street. "Semi bullets?"

"It's a work in progress."

On the other side of Beverly Hills, we pulled in for gas at a Signal station next to a trampoline farm. At least, that's what I called those places where kids paid a quarter to bounce around for twenty minutes, turn flips, and come close to breaking their necks. The accident insurance must have been enormous—assuming they even had any.

The service station was in the midst of a gas war, so we got a free set of steak knives and a quart bottle of Coke with our nineteen-cents-per-gallon fill-up. We drove under an overpass and, farther up Santa Monica Boulevard, I cut over at Melrose Avenue past Vine to park out on the street in front of Nickodell's restaurant.

Norm and I got out and strolled over to the main, arched entrance of my favorite movie studio, Paramount, home to Henry Aldrich, Hopalong Cassidy, and "Road" movies. Chandler had worked on *Double Indemnity* here, and even appeared on screen in a cameo role. Ah, they didn't make 'em like they used to.

Like Norman, I knew a guy who knew a guy here, only my guy was the current gate guard, Fritz Hawkes, so we got in easy—with a folded ten dollar bill. Thank God, I still had some of Wayne's pocket money, or I'd be getting writer's cramp when it came time to make out an expense report for this case.

Norm dashed off to see someone he knew in the prop department, leaving me just inside the gate with Hawke.

I chatted with Fritz the gate guard while he chewed gum in a way that made his jowls wobble. There were a lot of folds in his face, so it was interesting to watch. I told him I was looking for Caesar Silverman, and he made a quick phone call to pass the word along.

"Silverman used to be a vice president at the Dumont network, before it went bankrupt and shut down in '55," he ruminated and swallowed.

"I know. I did a piece of work on the old Captain Video set. Some kid stole a toy ray-gun." I didn't say it was how I'd first met Norman.

"Paramount invested heavily in television back then and stayed away ever since. You'll find him two streets up and to the left in one of the production bungalows."

I thanked him as an ape-man and a showgirl strolled past with a wave. Following them down a narrow alley between two blimp-hanger-sized sound stages, I began to question whether or not I was dreaming. What did I expect to accomplish by being here, dodging between extras dressed as cowboys, centurions, and cops? And what exactly was this case about, anyway?

Was I out to save the world or after revenge? Did I think I'd find a lead to Dr. Z, or a dead end? Was I in my right mind, or another illusion from that damned drug? I realized that those sorts of questions mirrored just about every case I'd handled during the last year.

Again, I wondered what Mr. P, my mentor, would have done. But Mr. P was far away, retired, and sipping Pepsi through a straw on some sunny Hawaiian beach, no doubt, while I was pounding the backlot pavement, searching for clues and tramping up the three wooden steps that lead to the bungalow office door of Production VP Caesar Silverman.

I knocked and went in without waiting.

"Who?" a middle-aged man in a nice head of graying hair and a sleeveless, diamond-patterned sweater shouted at a speaker phone. "Mansfield? The girl with the knock out knockers? I'll get back to you on that." He punched a button on the phone and popped a filter-tipped cigarette into his wide mouth, ignoring my presence.

Staring down at the desk where the phone sat, he began patting his pants and jacket pockets, searching for a light.

I got out my courtesy Zippo and passed him a flame.

He puffed a couple of times and let the Viceroy hang from his lips. "And you are?"

I snapped the lighter shut and put it away. "Looking for Silverman."

He didn't let that bother him. "Now, Mr..." He glanced down at a slip of paper on his polished desktop "...Reilly. I'm sorry. I didn't catch your first name. And please don't say, 'I didn't throw it.'"

This guy was quite the card. Keeping my lips as straight as uncooked spaghetti, I said, "Doghouse."

He continued talking as if I'd never answered, "Well I've only a few minutes—Doghouse?"

"It's a pet name. My girl gave it to me when we were joking around one evening."

His grimace said that I'd gone too far with the gag. "I'm Mr. Silverman, but I'm through here for the moment. You can make an appointment or…"

I waited to see if his next words would be "go to hell" or "drop dead". They were neither.

"…wait in the other office until I return." He grabbed a felt hat and swiveled around the edge of his gleaming desk.

"You don't have an outer office."

As he went past me, he spoke in a low voice. "My point exactly."

I had been bested. Game, set, and match.

Out again in the warming sun, I watched Silverman hoof it around the corner of Stage Seven, just as Norman, wearing 3-D glasses, strolled up with another guy. The other guy was Jerry Lewis.

The red and blue plastic lenses reflected back at me. "Here's your new gun," he smiled, handing me a blue-black S&W .38.

To a certain extent, the two men could have passed for twins. Norm wore glasses underneath his 3-D specs, but otherwise in hair style, facial dimension, height, weight, and loose, limber stance, he could have passed for the long lost brother of Jerry Lewis.

I accepted the gun, squeezing it between my belt and the small of my back, under my coat. Lewis didn't seem to mind at all and offered a hand. "Any friend of the Professor, here, is a friend of mine."

"I've been inventing devices that Mr. Lewis can use in *Cinderfella*," Norm beamed. "Special electronic explosions and stuff."

I shifted my eyes to Jerry. "I thought you were making that science fiction movie, *Visit to a Tiny Planet*, or something."

"Nah, we wrapped that and I'm producing my own projects now. *Cinderfella* is the first one in a two-pic-per-year deal—if Disney doesn't sue over the title. It's going to be a really, really big shoo, thanks to our nutty friend here."

Norm mocked one of Lewis's famous takes of alarm, "Here now!"

Lewis snickered and gave my pal's shoulder a shove.

"Anyway," Norm almost gushed, "I got you that gun you needed, so you can keep after the bad guys now."

I was conscious of the extra weight at the base of my spine. "And I appreciate it, but I've got to get after Silverman."

"Caesar?" Lewis looked at his wristwatch. I noticed that even now, off stage, he wore French cuffs and links. "He's probably over at his table in the commissary. Come on. I'll learn ya."

❧❧❧

The place was as crowded and busy as the Alamo during the siege. There was a long counter with serving pans of food and stacks of trays along one wall of the room. A couple of dozen groupings of tables and chairs were filled with off-duty film people yakking and eating. It was a lot like being back at the Brown Derby, what with all the familiar faces feeding their…well, faces.

The tantalizing sweet-sour smell of sauerkraut bit through my clogged sinuses. As we settled into an empty table in the back, I recognized Benson Fong lunching with John Carradine. And I saw Silverman's erect figure seated near the food line, talking with another guy who seemed vaguely familiar from the back.

"That's Silverman over there," I told Norm, keeping my head down and a hand in front of my face for make-shift concealment. "Go on over and get in line. See if you can hear what they're talking about."

A card in the center of our table, propped up by the salt and pepper shakers, told about Today's Specials. I picked it up, positioning it in a way that helped hide my features.

Lewis seemed fascinated. "Secret super spy. I get it."

Norm stood in line between Jack Oakie and Juliet Prowse, but I could tell he was trying to overhear Silver-man's conversation. Tony Perkins came in and, for a moment, it was like looking in a mirror. We could have been brothers.

Lewis apparently noticed me staring. "He's working on some Hitchflick cock. Get it?"

Norm came back to our table with coffee and three slices of velvet cake on a tray, just as Ramon Navarro was leaving.

"Whad he say?" Lewis asked.

Norman folded up his 3-D glasses and slipped them into his shirt pocket. No one here took the slightest notice before or after. "He said they had the money now and they'd be able to finalize production and release it in the next few days."

"Must be working on some new picture deal," Jerry mused, forking a wedge of cake.

The coffee tasted like it had been laced with 10W30. The back of that guy's head was beginning to bug me—and then I realized why. He wasn't just some guy, he was my guy. I spoke in amazement: "Guy Lombard."

"Nah," Lewis said. "He don't work here. Why would an old bandleader be—"

I cut him off by coming to my feet and inadvertently jostling the table. A few people took notice, including Silverman. Lombard caught his expression and turned in his seat to stare back at me. Then the two of them made for the exit.

Norm and Jerry ran behind me as I rushed to the door. In the bright sunlight, I watched Silverman and Lombard split up, each heading in a different direction, down separate alley-ways between sound stages. "You guys go after that guy and I'll go after this guy," I ordered, thinking that I needed to expand my vocabulary.

As near as I could tell, Lombard and I were headed for the back of the backlot. I ran about thirty feet behind him with one hand at my lower back, holding the gun in place. He should have been dead, drowned in the 'Frisco Bay. Maybe he had a twin? From another dimension?

There was a massive sliding door in the high back wall of the studio grounds beneath the tall water tower. It was like a huge barn-door on a long rail of over-head rollers. Some wag had painted it with large block letters that read: KEY POUT!

Lombard had gotten the door to slide open enough so he could slip through. I squeezed after him, coming up quickly to a cautious stop, expecting him to be waiting on the other side with a two-by-four or a chunk of concrete. I was lucky this time and didn't get my head ambushed.

Off in the distance, my guy was running a marathon down a gravel lane, across a plot of freshly-mowed grass, between the gray, hip-high gravestones.

The sight stalled me for a sec. Then I came to realize where we were. The Hollywood Memorial Cemetery butted up against the back side of Paramount Studios. The joke was that here was where the film company execs came for lunch, spading over the dirt of their predecessors and other famous folk, munching on the brittle bones of old celebs and actors.

The reality was that the cemetery had been here long before the studio and both had over the years prospered and expanded until they'd met in an uncomfortable détente—the world of the dead connected to the world of dreams. Or was it the other way around?

But all that was just another ancient Hollywood legend. What mattered now was that I had to get my ass moving again. I ran forward, under fifty-foot tall palms in the direction of the Hollywood sign far off in the hazy distance.

Guy veered to the left, heading toward one of the mausoleums. I hustled after, my footfalls crunching on the gravel like dry toast. Inside the marble edifice, the air was cooler and now my footsteps echoed off the glossy white walls. I began tiptoeing in order not to be heard, feeling like an idiot.

I passed the crypts of Constance and Norma Talmadge in the aisle called the Sanctuary of Peace. Farther down was what would someday be the final resting place of Clifton Webb, good old Waldo Lydecker of *Laura*.

I heard a crashing sound, like the front of a grandfather clock being smashed or in a vase impacting the stone floor.

I doubled back, drawing out my gun, and came to a cross passage. I cut over to another aisle, thinking the noise had come from that direction. To say that this place was creepy didn't do it justice.

Guy or Joe Lombard was down on his knees in front of a smashed-in crypt. From my angle, it looked like he was reaching in and pulling out bundles of cash. The bills were wrapped in dull red bank bands and seemed almost new as he shoved them into his suit coat pockets.

I slowly approached his stooped form. "What does it take to kill you?"

He paused, slumped his broad shoulders, and then looked at me with mustard-yellow eyes. "I was going to ask the same thing, Wade."

"That's Mr. Wade. Get up. Slow."

He complied, but not to the last word. I'd forgotten how fast he was.

He flipped a bundle of cash at me and the movement drew my aim off enough that he could ram the top of his head into my own valuables.

We went down together just like in a Republic serial. I kicked out and missed.

He swung at my head and grazed my left temple.

I clutched and ripped his coat sleeve.

He got hold of my gun, and yanked it from my hand.

A small group of mourners came into the Sanctuary of Light, attracted by our disturbance. The same look of fear and desperation that I'd seen several times before etched their faces. Mine, too, probably.

Lombard pointed my new .38 down at me. "All those people are going to be killing each other in forty-eight hours."

I started to get to my feet.

"But, you'll die now, Wade." He pulled the trigger and fired into my right leg.

I felt the impact and cried out as he fired again, hitting my other leg. I went down in searing pain.

Through blurred vision, I watched helpless as the crowd scattered and Lombard said, "Try and chase me now," as he slipped away past Jesse Lasky's tomb.

CHAPTER 21

asky had died last year, only a few months before his old partner DeMille. Together, the two men had produced the first full length movie in Hollywood, *The Squaw Man*, and had founded the company that later became Paramount. I couldn't say why such nonsense ran through my mind after I'd been shot. I must have been in shock.

I wasn't dead yet. But I was in stupendous pain. So much pain that I almost envied Lasky. Almost.

I lay there, unable to get up. Both my legs felt sawed off above the knee.

I fought not to black out. Above my head was an exclamation point. I was writhing in pain under the burial vault of John "Bert" Adams, catcher for the Phillies, who had died in 1940. On the front of his crypt was a baseball bat and ball.

Feeling a lot like Felix the Cat, I grabbed the bat and used it as a crutch to raise myself on wobbly legs to an upright position.

And that's how things stood, as Norm and Jerry Lewis came around the corner.

"Holy hell," Lewis yelped.

Norm got his shoulder under my armpit. "Mr. Wade, good thing he shot you."

"Bull shit," I groaned, and tried to limp forward.

Lewis got under my other arm and we staggered outside. "He should be bleeding like a stuck swine. Why isn't he bleeding?"

Norm set me on a stone bench and inspected my trousers. "The gun had rubber bullets. It's one of my new inventions for making movies safer."

I massaged the ache in my thighs. "Rubber bullets?"

Lewis stood there and repeated the words, as a siren began to wail in the distance.

"Well," Norman told us, "at least I didn't use silver."

I swung at him, saying, "Ha, ha."

He easily ducked away as Jerry mused, "*The Lone Wolfman.*"

Like I said, they were a lot alike.

The siren got louder as a patrol-car bounced onto the ground through the main entrance on Santa Monica. A few long minutes later, an officer of the law strode up and stared at us through mirrored sunglasses. "All right. Who wants to explain all this?"

Norm immediately pointed at me, but before I could speak, Lewis took the cop aside for a friendly chat.

I looked down and saw that I was seated near the grave of Bugsy Siegel. "Did you happen to see which way Lombard went?"

Norm replied. "Ah—who?"

"Great! What happened to the moneyman you were chasing, Silverman?"

"Ah—we lost him. But we know where he lives."

I gave my legs a test. It still hurt like hell, but I could stand. "He won't be there. But we should check it out anyway."

Dean's ex-partner came back without the cop.

I watched as the patrol-car cruised slowly away and breathed easier. Somewhere above me a little bird tweeted. For real.

Norm pushed his glasses up with his index finger and asked Lewis, "What did you tell him?"

Jerry helped me limp back toward the studio. "I gave him a couple of free tickets and said it was all a scene from my next feature film. Maybe it will be. The cops in this town are very understanding."

"That hasn't been my experience," I replied.

"No worries, chum. Just take it easy. Hey, there's a stage doctor in the admin building. Let's get you looked at."

"Okay. Thanks to both of you. But next time, can I get a gun with real bullets?"

৵৩৵৩

As predicted, we were unable to locate Caesar Silverman. We did find out, however, that he'd been siphoning off cash from the Production Department's budget, and would be arrested if, and when, he could be located. I figured that, given the facts of the case, he was now south of the border, down Mexico way.

I took the remainder of the day to try and heal my sore legs. I had welts and bruises there that made my earlier black eyes look like hickies.

Norm drove me back to my boat, after the studio doc gave me a packet of Darvon for my pain. Just what I needed—more drugs.

I snacked on left-over bacon and eggs and fell into a solid, sound sleep, only to be shaken gently from my bunk and introduced to Candy

৵৩৵৩

She wore her long blonde hair in a ponytail. She was cute and a little plump for my tastes, but she was Norm's girlfriend, not mine. She was also all business in her manner, studying to be a virologist, or micro-biologist, or something.

Over the next ten minutes, while I noticed that there was a slight leak forming below decks in the aft portion of my boat, we discussed what little I knew of Dr. Z's drug—its compound and effects, as well as its potential threat.

There wasn't much that I understood about medicine or drugs, as such. I took an aspirin or Darvon when I had a ripping headache and cough syrup when I had a sore throat. The two together sometimes made me dizzy, but in no way were they addictive, right?

I knew people who had acquired a golden arm, and I'd helped them get down off the horse with an intervention for their own good. But none of this prepared me for an understanding of what Dr. Z had claimed to have created.

It was some sort of addictive hallucinogenic, causing a contagious disease. From it, you could get slap happy and see things that weren't there—or as Phil Dick claimed, were there, but you weren't supposed to see— while spreading the condition to other people simply by breathing in their direction.

I'd heard of mass hysteria, but this was the first time I'd encountered a chemical way of causing it.

Even though I didn't pretend to understand a lot of this bio-med stuff, I kept my face blank as she explained about the power and glory of Indian hemp, mescaline from Mexican peyote, and various forms of lysergic acid.

She took time to draw out a diagram of ethyl-methyl-chicken-wire and managed to convince Norman, at least, that the thing made sense. Conspiracy nut that he was, Norm became quite concerned. "Only a few years ago, the government conducted biological warfare tests, releasing whooping cough bacteria in Tampa Bay, causing an epidemic, and killing twelve people."

I seemed to recall hearing about that and looked at the girl for confirmation, waiting for the bottom-line and the fine print at the end.

"This has got to be stopped," she concluded. "The result could be catastrophic. Especially, if this designed drug becomes aerosolized and combines with all the chlorofluorocarbons in our air from the Freon in air-conditioners. You've got to let me help stop this."

Damn. My legs hurt.

"You know, she can lead us to water," Norm said, "but I don't want her going there to drink."

I understood his feelings. "I think that's a sound idea."

She was still all business. "You're going to need me in order to identify the process. How else will you know how to stop it?"

"When the time comes, we can just kick it over."

"And get it all over you?" she protested. "What if it gets loose in the atmosphere? Weren't you listening just now? This has got to be handled properly, chemically. This has the potential of being a mass bio-weapon, especially if it combines with sulfur dioxide or carbon monoxide."

The hair on the back of my neck creeped up. "You mean…"

She nodded, emphatically. "The smog."

Norman placed his hands on the top of his head as if to hold it there. "Can't we just throw acid on it or something?"

She glared at him and then me, too.

"No," Norm said, "I guess not."

The leak in my boat's hull would have to wait.

CHAPTER 22

The next morning, Wednesday, October, twenty-first, an odd team of individuals assembled in the offices of Sunset Investigations on the sixth floor of the Taft Building on Hollywood Boulevard.

The call had gone out the previous evening to meet in Suzi's offices by ten-thirty a.m.

Sunset Eye had been incorporated five years earlier by Suzi's then husband, Johnny.

Unlike me, he'd been a hot-shot, hip, and handsome businessman, who'd established a reputation for discretion and results. I was discrete in my investigations too, but I never got the kind of results he did—including the final result that got him dead.

I hadn't encountered Suzi after her marriage until

earlier this year while she was snooping out what had happened to her missing husband. After we'd uncovered the truth, she had drifted back to me and gradually decided to continue operating the agency, partly out of revenge and partly as a way to give me a shot at Johnny's old client list.

Within six months, she had not only revived the business, she had excelled at it.

Now, in her new digs, I limped off the elevator and found that she'd hired another old friend to act as receptionist.

"Hi, Weezie. Remember me?"

The freckled, honey-colored blonde with the deep tan smiled up at me and removed her telephone headset. "Sure do, Mr. Wade. Actually, you were the one who introduced me to Lloyd, but don't tell his wife."

"Ah…okay." The last time I saw Louise Parker she had been working out at Marineland, where we'd solved a murder and located some hundred-year-old sunken treasure. Now she sat here in a tastefully furnished lobby that smelled of fresh paint and contained some old guy patiently waiting on a low sofa behind a lower coffee table covered with fresh copies of *Time*, *Newsweek*, and *The Saturday Review*. Seated next to him, I thought I recognized Mike Romanoff, and I wondered why the most outrageous phony in the phony capital of the world thought he needed a private investigations firm.

"This is our newest operative, Mr. Wade," Weezie

said, as a young ivy-leaguer with sandy hair and penetrating blue eyes walked up from an interior hallway. "Bradford Westfield."

Right off the bat, he reminded me of Paul Newman. Probably graduated from Hollywood High and knew a lot of young stars. From his physique, I guessed he played tennis, surfed, and body-built. I would have called him "Moose," if I wasn't afraid he'd crush me.

He smiled, gripping and shaking my right hand. "Suzi tells me you think Noir films are all about style, rather than content."

We'd only met seconds ago, and he wanted to argue esthetics. "Started with German Expressionism," I responded, "and took a dive down into flashing neon signs and striped shadows from Venetian blinds."

"You're wrong. Noir is about some poor sap who is deceived, usually by a dame, until he chooses to kill against his better judgment."

I felt my drug-induced anger rising. At least, I thought it was drug-induced. I tamped it down. "You'd do anything for Suzi, wouldn't you?"

"Wouldn't you?"

Norman stuck his head around the corner from down that mean hallway and motioned, mouthing, "Come here."

Moose and I stared into each other's brains for a second longer. Then he broke it off and we walked in my pal's direction.

We came into a paneled conference room and found chairs around a long, gleaming oak table. There was a movie screen that I learned Norman had installed which lowered from the ceiling on a small buzzing motor.

Suzi looked smart and sharply-dressed in a dark blue skirt with matching vest over a crisp white blouse. The business outfit set off her trim blonde hair and flashing eyes. They flashed my way, and I could feel them burning a hole in my heart.

I looked away and saw Lex, Candy, Norm, and the new kid, Brad, all settling in as Suzi took a seat and said to me, "Go."

I didn't take it that she wanted me to leave, but to bring everyone up to date with what I knew about the threat posed by Dr. Z.

It went something like this:

"Based on the cash Lombard got from the stash in the crypt, I think Silverman was money man, organizing funding for the Saint Anthony Foundation that Zachariah Cortina mentioned to me."

Suzi returned my full gaze. "That's the group that's driving production of the drug, somewhere?"

"Yep. Somewhere."

Candy drew her chair closer to the table. "It would be somewhere cool enough to control the production and avoid accidental exposure."

Norm nodded agreement. "So we're looking for a cold place, like an ice rink or a refrigerated meat locker…"

My head was starting to hurt again and I could feel the anger beginning to build up. I worked to keep it under control. "It would be someplace bigger than that. I'd guess. A place where they wouldn't be disturbed. Also, they'd have backup generators to maintain electric power if there ever was a failure."

"There must be dozens of places like that in the LA basin," Lex groused.

I sat there massaging my left knee before it cramped again. "But you're forgetting that they're depending on the weather patterns to carry the damned drug deep into the smog layer."

"So that means—" Suzi continued the thought. "—they'd likely want it to flow down into—"

"Flow down from someplace in the mountains," Lex said.

"Where it would be cold," Candy added.

"It can start snowing like mad up around Mt. Baldy, this time of year," Brad told us.

"More importantly," I thought out loud, "Mt. Baldy is actually the San Antonio Mountain." I slammed my fist down and a large metallic ashtray in the center of the table bounced from the impact. "That's it, goddammit!" I felt my breathe shorten in an attack of anger or panic. "We're looking for a son-of-a-bitching self-powered lab up on Mt. Baldy."

They all stared at my rage.

I had to get out of there, before I said or did something even more harmful. I hobbled back to the reception area and concentrated on staring out a window that was partly blocked by the cross-cross spider web of an iron fire-escape.

As a further distraction, I used the phone to place a long-distance call to information and finally got Philip K. Dick on the line.

"I'm fine," he said. "How are you hanging?"

My hand shook, and I felt like I was running a raging temperature. "So, you're recovering well? That's good. That's promising. What's your trick?"

"Get all the milk and orange juice you can," he advised. "It'll flush the drug out of your system and set you straight." He said it also helped to read a Zen book by a guy named Watts, called *Be Here Now*.

I wasn't sure I heard that last part correctly.

My buddy, Norm, came out of the conference room and gave me a questioning look.

"Hold on a minute, Phil. I've got someone here who'd like to speak with you." I handed the receiver to Norm and whispered, "Philip K. Dick."

His eyelids shot up as he grabbed at the phone, almost dropping it in his excitement.

I stepped away quickly enough to avoid the emotional explosion. The sight of Norm's enthusiasm did my soul good.

Then Brad came over to me. "I want to talk with you about Suzi."

Oh, brother. This was a conversation that was sure to calm me down. Yeah, right.

He squared off against me again. "She deserves better than a low-life beach bum."

Norman had his hand over the phone receiver. "He says he had a dream where you were a character in a series of popular mystery/adventure novels," he called to me. "There was a guy in Ohio who was published the stories electronically on a 'world of web' or something."

I felt my fists clinging at my sides and swallowed a gallon of hate. I tensed further, slowly turned away from Brad, and walked very carefully back into the meeting room.

♥♥♥

Weezie followed me, bringing the office copy of a *Thomas Brothers Guide* and Suzi went down to her car to get a Shell gas-station roadmap from her glove compartment. Brad followed her.

I scanned the room, gradually getting full control of my rage. I noticed something strange. No one here smoked. For this, I and my sinuses were grateful.

When Suzi and Brad got back, he was popping a breath mint into his mouth and she edged over my way, asking me to "step outside."

I sucked in a deep breath and complied. *Here we go again.*

We went back to her office which over-looked the corner of Vine and Hollywood. It occurred to me that we were only two blocks east of where Chandler had placed Philip Marlowe's offices.

She stepped close to me. "I've got something in my eye."

This sounded inviting. "Let me look."

She backed away, abruptly. "Never mind. I've got it now."

"I see. Then you don't need me, after all?"

She picked up a stainless steel letter opener from her desk.

Now I backed away. Then embarrassed, I came back to my original position.

She spoke between clinched teeth. "You leave Brad alone. And you don't ever raise your hand to me again. Ever."

My anger dissolved immediately. "Look. I'm sorry. I didn't mean—"

"*Ever.*"

I swallowed. "Ever. Got it. Never again."

"I mean it. I'll have you arrested and put away." She opened a desk drawer and put the knife inside. "He's just a boy. A loyal—"

"Puppy?"

"He likes old movies like you. He's done a lot of in-vestigation into the local communist cells. I thought you two would hit it off."

"Well, again, I'm sorry, but I don't like him."

"Seems like you don't like anyone much anymore. It's really eating at you, isn't it?"

It was a fair, good question. And I didn't have a good answer—yet. But I nodded.

Her smile brightened and she touched the engagement ring on her finger. "I love you, Standy."

I came over and pulled her to me, enjoying her warmth, her lips, and her tender embrace.

We held each other for a quiet moment.

"I promise," I said into her hair. "I'll never to hurt you again."

She leaned back and looked up at me questioningly. "Because…"

"Because I love you, too."

"That's right."

I let her pull free and go back to her desk. She opened another drawer and took out a hefty silver-plated automatic.

When she handed it to me, it felt like it would have the firepower of a howitzer. "Here. You'll be needing some protection."

That could have been an invitation to a little skewering, but I didn't chance it.

"That's swell, sweetheart," I said in a non-Bogart voice and checked to be sure that this gun was loaded with real ammo. "Uh…you got any milk?"

She smiled at me and I felt great! "Sure. I'll get you some. Now. What's the deal with this nurse Rosita?"

I gulped loud enough to have it appear on the Rector scale.

CHAPTER 23

When we came back into the meeting room, we found that the others had the maps spread out over the conference table.

Suzi consulted a city directory and made a phone call to the reference room of the public library to get the address and location information of the San Antonio Foundation. "It looks like it's here in the winter sports area next to Cucamonga Park."

"Then, we'll have to take 66 over to Route 30," I answered, consulting the road map, "past the San Antonio dam and up Mount Baldy road."

"Looks like they're over in San Bernardino County, instead of Los Angeles," Brad commented, drumming his fingers on the table top. "Clever devils. That'll confound us getting support from the local sheriff."

"And, is that federal land?" Suzi wondered. "Who has jurisdiction up there?"

"It might as well be on the back side of the moon," Norm said.

"We should go up there and reconnoiter, probably at night so they won't see us."

Lex cleared her throat. "Who are us?"

Before I could answer, Norm adjusted his glasses and shook his head to the side like Jimmy Durante. "Night on Mount Baldy! Walt would love it! Va-va-va-voom!"

As usual, he had a good point and made the most of it. Maybe it *was* time to enlist Walt's help. I wondered how long it would take to get that help. I wondered how much time we had, period. "Is that a Farmer's Almanac you have there?" I asked Lex.

"Yeah." She flipped the pages. "And it says the winter winds are predicted to sweep down harshly this season."

"When does the season begin?"

"October twentieth. Yesterday."

"Time to go," Norm said.

Suzi raised her hands for calm. "Let's not be hasty."

I winced.

"Let's review what we know and what we can possibly do," she went on.

Again, we pinpointed the location of the institute on the map. The elevation this time of year would ensure that the temperature stayed below freezing there. They would have an ideal environment for the manufacture of the "stuff" and, when they released it, it would look like a simple snow squall coming down from the mountains to combine with the smog.

"I'm getting an image of an avalanche of death," Brad said.

"It's a chilling thought," Lex agreed in her frog voice.

Candy estimated that, if conditions were right, two hours after the release, tens of thousands of Los Angelinos would be infected by Dr. Z's drug. And if the Santa Anna winds blew up from the southeast, the deadly cloud could be trapped over the LA basin for days, turning it into a hell-hole full of innocent but raging murderers.

This was far worse than anything I'd ever imagined from a book or experienced in any movie.

"A million Jack the Rippers rioting," Norm said,

"There's never been anything like it," Suzi agreed, holding a palm to the side of her lovely face. "Thousands of normal people turning savagely on one another. Ordinary citizens attacking and killing each other. Regardless of age, sex, or race."

"LA becoming a gigantic slaughterhouse," Candy said in soft awe.

"And who knows if it'll stop there?" I turned to the micro-bio girl. "What if some of the infected people manage to travel to Palm Springs, or San Diego, or—"

"Or a military base?" Lex coughed.

Norm's girlfriend slumped her shoulders.

"Should we alert the newspapers, radio and TV stations?" asked the Moose. "Should we call out the national guard, or the FBI?"

"I don't think we have time. Lombard bragged yesterday that in less than forty-eight hours, we'd all be killing each other. That means we've got to move fast. It could happen any time today."

"Lemme see that map again," Norman said. "Where is that institute?"

We all looked over his shoulder. Far up on the right-hand corner of the chart, we could see a winding road that led up to Mount San Antonio.

"According to a couple of biker buddies I know—" Lex grumbled.

"Hell's Angles?" Candy asked.

"—it's here near Glendora Ridge Road. We could set up a base camp at the dam and go in under cover of night."

"If we live to see the night and work together to stop them," Suzi said.

"The JLLA," Norm said.

"The what?" Candy asked.

"The Justice Legion of LA. We'll stop them!"

"You've been reading way too many comic books," Lex and I both said.

"New ones at the drug store every Tuesday and Thursday."

I thought again about how good it was to be back home among the usual gang of idiot friends.

"It's a heavily forested area," Suzi was saying. "Secluded, but with one side clearly facing the valley below. The stuff will have no trouble rolling down into the basin and spreading, smothering the city. Who are these people again? Do they have a lot of guns?"

"I did some checking," Brad bragged. "They're a radical, racist organization quietly backed by the Communist Party, from down south of the border, where our government can't touch them. We have no jurisdiction down there, of course, but that doesn't stop their group from coming up here and funding operation against us."

"So if we cut off their head on Mt. Baldy," Norm said, "what's to keep them from growing another someplace else and launching an attack all over again?"

"Not much, I'm afraid," I responded. "But the next time, we'd be prepared and possibly expecting it."

"We're expecting it now," Lex admitted.

Candy shrugged. "But they'd still need someone who knows how to correctly formulate the substance."

I thought of Rosita. "And they'd still need the proper geographical location, full of smog, like our fair little Los Angeles, eh?"

"More and more cities in the USA are starting to struggle with reduced air quality," the young girl reminded us. "If things don't change with formaldehyde in our paints and fluorocarbons in our plastic cups, in a decade or so, conditions could allow them to strike almost any populated area."

"Sobering thought, that," Lex croaked,

"So, how do we get up there?" Suzi asked. "Who all goes? And in what vehicle from which direction?"

"Can we parachute in?"

Candy punched Norm's arm. Hard.

"Whatever we decide," Suzi said, "Brad stays here."

"What?" asked several of us, including Brad.

"Did you see those clients in the waiting room?" She pointed at the closed conference room door. "And we've got that new political scandal case with the Honorary Mayor of Van Nuys."

"Andy Devine?" Lex asked, sounding just like him.

"Yes, but—" Brad almost whined.

"You'll have backup. I've contracted with that other PI, Eliot Cross, for a few days' work."

"Not that guy—" I protested, but Weezie opened the meeting room door and stuck her head in before I could finish my statement.

"There's a very weird woman out here who wants to see you, Mr. Wade."

"Weirder than Weirick?" Lex barked.

Norm started to punch her in the shoulder, but thought better of it.

"Who is it now?" I asked.

"She says her name—"

Before she could finish, an accented voice called from behind her, "Rosita Fey De Silva."

CHAPTER 24

S he wore an emerald green dress, trim and long, held with a glossy black belt. At her throat was a leopard-print scarf and her hair was done up high with lots of swirls.

The introductions were long and tricky, especially with Suzi. We really didn't have the time for much conversation. She said she'd escaped while Dr. Z and Lombard were busy with the formula, but I was more interested in learning how she'd found me here. When I asked, she said I'd mentioned Suzi Sunset when I was unconscious.

"But I don't talk in my sleep," I protested emphatically.

I saw Suzi nodding her head emphatically.

I stood erect on my sore legs and cleared my throat. "Okay. Here's what we're going to do. Norm, I need some sort of camera or electronic bug to capture evidence against Dr. Z's operations."

"Right."

"We'll need a large quantity of a chemical base to nullify the acidic properties of the drug," Candy said. "Assuming we can get near enough to apply it."

"I can get plenty of Ajax cleanser from the back of Sonny's restaurant, if that'll work," Lex grumbled.

"That just might do the trick," Candy answered. "And it would be a good idea if we could get some tear gas to use against any escaping vapors."

Suzi tapped the tip of a lead pencil on the table top. "Good. Because we need to alert the police, anyway."

"All right. Anything else?" I looked pointedly at Brad, who remained mum. "Then, let's plan to meet up at the reservoir before dark. Rosita, you go with Norm and me."

෧෨

There was a long, ugly scar on my left cheek and a line of dark stitches along my brow. The skin of my face gleamed with grease and the rubbery tang of Latex filled my nostrils.

Norm had applied his monster makeup kit to make us look like a cross between south-sea Lascars and Mexican banditos. He'd had fun over-doing it as we needed a disguise to get past any guards who might challenge us. I just wished he hadn't made himself resemble the wolf-man so much.

"The rethavoir thould be right on the leff," he said around cheeks stuffed with cotton balls, one of which he spat onto the floorboard of my Thunderbird.

The snow had begun to fall about a half-hour earlier and was already a good inch thick.

We met Suzi and Lex at the dam and transferred three heavy pails of gray cleaning powder to the trunk of my car. Through a set of binoculars, Lex watched farther up the road.

Mt. Baldy was a white pyramid in the distance over 10,000 feet high. Off in the other direction, down the two-lane highway collecting with gathering flakes, I could still catch a glimpse of the hazy valley and its semi-innocent city.

"There's a couple a trucks on this side of the tunnel," Lex reported. "I can't see any markings on their sides, but the motors are running, so someone's up there waitin' for something."

"They're probably trying to keep warm." Suzi hugged herself. "I don't blame them. This storm is worse than expected."

"And it's early in the season," Rosita added.

Suzi glared at her. "How, exactly, would you know that?"

"I know more than you think, Mizz Sunset."

"We've got to get moving, folks," I said, in order to defuse the growing nuclear detonation between the two women. "If those really are guards up ahead, Norm and I will pretend to be bringing Rosita back to the Foundation. The rest of you hang loose here."

They didn't much like my strategy, but they did as I suggested.

I drove the T-bird up toward the black mouth of the tunnel. The men there were indeed guards, although not of any official capacity. As we approached, a burly gorilla got out of one of the trucks and raised a gloved hand for us to stop.

We gave him our story about bringing Rosita back to Dr. Z. He leered at her, smiled, and nodded. She knew him, but he didn't know us. And the soft rubber on Norm's nose seemed slightly longer than the last time I looked. Despite the lowering temperature around us, the latex on his face was slowly melting.

Burly spoke into a handy-talky while we kept our peace. I didn't see any guns, but there were plenty of places where they could be stashed in the trucks and the bulky jackets that the guards wore.

The guard stepped back, patted the car's roof, and waved us on.

We drove through the gathering snow and into the tunnel that stretched darkly perhaps a thousand yards to come out into a spectacular view. A steep drop over-looked a lush valley full of snow-capped yellow pines and white firs. A couple hundred feet farther down, I saw a full-grown buck watch us pass, before it bounded into the brush.

One of the trucks crept up on our tail, trailing us up the steep, slippery road.

"Did you plan on us being followed, Mr. Wade?"

I didn't have an answer, so I kept driving until we came to a second tunnel. This one was shorter than the first and the truck didn't follow us through. That was the good news. The bad news was that there was yet another truck on the other side that we passed as we came out of the darkness.

I down shifted into second gear in order to increase traction on the glassy road and crept along, noting that the truck failed to follow.

Everyone in our car exhaled loudly.

I steered around a curve and brought the T-bird to a halt with the engine still running.

We hadn't seen a sign of any vehicles coming toward us down off the mountain. There were no tracks in the highway in front of us.

"Why are we stopping?" Rosita asked. "We're almost there."

"Yeah, Mr. Wade. What's wrong?"

"I don't like the feel of that left front tire. We may be getting a flat."

"Not now." The tip of Norm's nose wobbled and hung down nearly touching his upper lip.

"You better hop out and take a look," I told him.

"Okay." He stepped out the passenger-side door and walked around the front of the car, stooping for a sec and brushing the tire with his hand. Then, he came to the driver's window that I'd rolled down. "Looks all right to me."

I handed him Suzi's shiny automatic. "Here, you might need this."

My best buddy stared at the gun now in his hand. "What for?"

"Be careful with it, Norman." I stepped on the gas and skidded away, leaving him behind in the accumulating dim whiteness.

It was a dangerous thing to do—going off without a firearm.

Probably even more dangerous leaving one with Norm. But where I was headed, he would have found it even more dangerous, regardless of his confidence, cha, cha, cha.

Approximately five minutes farther up the inclined road, we came in sight of the Foundation's main building. The place was a little like something designed by Frank Lloyd Wright. Tucked under a copse of lodge-pole pines, there sat broad slabs of concrete stacked criss-cross, with one snow-covered wide terrace of stone jutting and hanging impossibly out over the valley below.

It reminded me of a site in Pennsylvania that I'd seen in pictures. *Falling Waters*. But there were also columns of Mexican Mayan blocks like in the Storer House down in LA. They'd filmed the *House on Haunted Hill* movie there a few months ago.

I didn't like it. The movie or our situation.

I pulled off the road and took the keys from the ignition. "You know," I told Rosita while leaning over her knees to unlock the glove compartment, "I can't fully trust you or your various stories."

Her dark eyes widened as I took out my back-up piece right in front of her lap.

"A lot of people think I'm stupid," I said, gesturing for her to get out of the car. "But I'm not."

"*Padrone, por favor—*"

"Don't start with that again, please."

"Why would you think I would lure you here? To what purpose?"

It was a fair question. I'd been running into a lot of those lately.

She didn't seem to know what else to say.

I pondered a moment longer, chewing the edge of my lower lip and finally pocketed the sidearm. "Come on."

Trudging through the ankle-high snow in our ordinary street shoes, we approached the low building. Too late, I saw a dark shape rise out of the freezing wall of grayness in front.

"That's far enough."

I wished to hell I'd been the one to say that.

"Up with the hands, Wade."

A snow flake hit me in the right eye while I watched a white rabbit scurry across the walkway and hide under the porch.

I wished to hell I'd been the one to do that.

CHAPTER 25

Even though night had pretty much fallen in the mountains, I could recognize who was confronting us. I would know that guy's voice anywhere.

"I'd guess you've got a gun." Lombard crunched down the snow-covered steps, moving toward me and holding what looked like a single-action .45.

"You'd guess right," I allowed reluctantly.

He grinned while patting me down again and found my .38.

"And, I'd reckon you've got a backup piece, too."

I watched the steam roll out of my mouth and dissolve into the gloom. "Of that, you'd be wrong."

Lombard patted me down some more in a lot of tender places. He found and took my scout knife. Then he patted down Rosita, seeming to take his time, enjoying the process.

"Inside."

He marched us through a foyer, a dusty hallway, down three steps to a large area with lots of clustered groupings of cushioned chairs that reminded me of a hospital waiting room. We went out a sliding glass door to a near-empty terrace that over-looked a wild low-land of snow-topped pines pointing into the gray sky. The air was brisk and I hoped he wouldn't throw us into it.

Dr. Z swung around to inspect us from where he'd been stooped over a contraption that looked like the insides of an air-conditioner with a few extra attachments.

My hands were raised, but that didn't stop me from rotating one like Queen Elisabeth. "What's up, Doc?"

He worked a kink out of his back and straightened his glasses. "Why do you persist, Mr. Wade? Most men today in your country cower from suspicion and fear of the enemy. Weakness from drugs and depression fill the American movie screens these days. Why are you so up-beat and can-do?"

"I come from a long history of American achievement." I tried to hide my frantic inventory of our surroundings with rambling words of gusto. "We fight for what's right. My heroes where those guys, like my brother, who fought the good fight and sometimes die for their country." A small table held a collection of tools, probably used during the construction of the doctor's infernal device, but the table was too far from me, over where Lombard held Rosita.

"When I was a kid, we had Navy Day to commemorate our fighting sailors." There were explosives attached to the dully-polished canister in his contraption. "We had powerful heroes in movie serials, comics, and detective magazines. All because we knew we had a job to do. And so do I."

"Who's this we?" Lombard called. "I don't see anyone else here but a half-crippled bum."

Dr. Z bent to set the countdown for the release of gas at sixty minutes.

"You don't understand," I replied over my shoulder. "We don't quit. And we win against the bad guys."

Z shook his head. Snow continued falling diagonally from the night sky behind him. "Remember, Mr. Wade, we don't control our lives. We just act like we do. I'm not a bad guy."

"Yes." I slumped and then straightened. "Yes, you are! You think you're as pure as the wind-driven snow, but you're not. You're the one who's full of unconscious prejudice. You don't think that you're a racist, but the proof is you tortured Slate and a host of Chinese people. You don't hate the White man, you hate everybody."

"That is just not true."

"Can I kill him now, Zach?" Lombard said,

There was a bottle of clear liquid on the table next to the pile of tools. Given that they were messing with explosives, I had a fair idea what it might be. "Let's review. You hate Whites, Blacks, American Indians, and Asians. Who do you like?"

Dr. Z raised a hand to indicate we should all listen carefully to what he had to say. "Me. I like me. And I like my brother. It's not about race, Mr. Wade. It's about brotherhood." He looked intently at Lombard and nodded.

"I'm going to kill him now," Guy growled. "But I want the woman for myself."

Dr. Z gave another fraction of a nod. "Take her, Joe. And then kill her, just like you did her brother."

I turned to face the man holding the gun.

Rosita's eyes were smeared, the darkest I'd ever seen them. "My brother?" she breathed beneath tears.

Another brother. Mine, Dr. Z's, and hers.

Lombard leered at her. "He died naked, begging."

Her eyes came back to me for a second, snapping with grim determination.

"No," I said. "Don't."

But her hand reached down and grasped the small bottle of clear liquid. In half a heartbeat, she slammed it into the side of Lombard's head, where it exploded with a deafening roar.

Dr. Z and I were kicked back through the glass doorway. My ears rang like the sound of a giant mosquito. I felt shards of glass crunching beneath me as I rolled over, attempting to get up.

Where Rosita and Lombard had stood, there was now a smoking jagged hole in the concrete deck. I watched a chunk of stone drop silently from the roof and fall into the mists in the valley below.

I knew I had to get to Z before he came to his senses. Stumbling toward his dark form, I saw him draw a gun from the folds of his coat and begin to swing it in my direction.

I was too far away to try and kick it from his hand, too sore and tired, too late.

He fired once, but the shot went high over my head.

I twisted to the right and ducked behind a chair.

Another shot went wild. I didn't hang around to find out where.

My right knee popped, but I got my feet under me and scrambled across the room and out a door.

I could hear Dr. Z shout something behind me, and was sure it included the phrase "give up."

Dazed and noticing a sharp pain in the right side of my neck. I took my hand away from the wet spot there and found in the dim light of the hallway a dark redness filling my palm.

I put my hand back on the slippery painful spot and applied pressure while shoving my way through a bulky door and into a laboratory like the one where I'd flunked Organic Chemistry class back at USC.

I was out of breath and unable to come to terms with the fact that Rosita had blown herself and Lombard to high hell. Why had I ever doubted her?

∾∾

He came after me. Cautiously moving in my direction. My blood trail was probably helping him. I tried to think of a way to use that to trick him, but I was becoming lightheaded.

"Mr. Wade," he called to me, as if I was Joel McCrea in *The Most Dangerous Game*.

Steam hissed from some device to my left. I crouched low, behind a lab table. Squat brown bottles with paper labels stood in a row on its marble surface.

"Come out, Mr. Wade. There is no other exit from this room." Dr. Z's voice sounded oh so rational and reasonable.

My mind fumbled along. What did I have in my pockets that I could use as a weapon against his gun? Maybe I could hit him between the eyes with my soggy shoe or my wallet or my courtesy lighter, or notebook. Stab him with my ball-point pen.

His footsteps were only…well, a few feet away, when I got a germ of an idea.

"Really, Mr. Wade." His voice held a disgruntled edge now. "We're running out of time."

I reached up and snagged one of the dark, glass-stopper bottles. Through the iron legs of the table, I saw his oxblood shoes turning in my direction.

An empty test tube tumbled end over end and bounced off my arm, shattering to the bare floor. He was toying with me.

"Ah, there you are, Mr. Wade."

I rose up to face him, which seemed to take him by surprise. But it wasn't enough to stop him from leveling the gun at my chest.

He was only a few feet away, so there was every chance that when he fired, he'd hit me dead center. "Now, hold still, Mr. Wade. This won't hurt a bit." His finger tightened on the trigger.

In what must have appeared as a feeble attempt to defend myself, I covered my face with my hand.

For half a second, he smiled. Then I sparked the Zippo lighter and spat a long flowing mouthful of ether at his rimless glasses. His head went up in gout of flame as big as a four-burner stove.

His face took on the aspect of an Edsel's front-end and began to turn reddish yellow. He fired his gun in wild directions, screaming and twisting his body, desperate to get away from the ball of fire.

I ducked down behind the marble table top, relishing the sound of a dozen Fay Wray's.

"Hijo de la chingada!" It was the first time I'd heard him speak his native language.

I shuffled behind his bent, smoking form and hobbled out the door, knowing that the flash of fire wouldn't permanently stop him.

My lips and tongue felt numb from holding in the mouthful of ether, but I knew I was smiling. How proud the Firewrangler would be when I told him this story.

If I told him this story. Right now, I was turned around lost, unsure where to go to find that bomb.

A profound weakness overcame my ability to navigate, let alone keep erect. I stumbled, fell, got up, lurched, swore, walked three steps to the left unintentionally and found that I was outside in more than a foot of snow.

I had trouble finding the building in all the whiteness. I had trouble finding my right arm. A numbness had set in that couldn't have been caused by the cold.

I could hear Dr. Z's hoarse voice yelling somewhere far in the distance. I wanted to be somewhere away from it, far in the distance, so I maneuvered around a large bush covered with loaves of snow. My breath seemed to blow out seven feet in front of my face.

I wondered if holding ether in your mouth would make you dizzy. Loss of blood could. I looked back and down and saw the trail of rouge I'd been leaving in the snow.

The storm had thickened. So had my brain.

Ice began to collect at the edges of my eyes and I could taste the cold. I thought I saw a large dark bat or bird swoop past my head and touch the white streak in my hair with its wing.

Another shape came toward me through the heavy grayness and I knew it was Dr. Zachariah Cortina. I began to shiver, telling myself it was from the cold.

I tried to move away, but found that I was trapped

between him and a drop-off that plunged down into a cloud of writhing whiteness. I saw that same rabbit, only he was white this time.

Dr. Z still carried his gun. I tried to make a snowball with my good hand, but all it got was a stony palm of cold wetness. The wind got even stronger, blowing snow in swirls and gusts that struck my face hard like sand. For a moment, I thought I was back in the desert. It sure as hell would have been warmer there.

I got up, feeling my knees crack again. One foot, two foot. Maybe if I backed away far enough, I could become lost in the howling snowstorm.

Fat black spots burst in front of my eyes. I'd lost a lot of blood and my vision was tunneling down.

I was mid-calf in snow now, out of breath, with teeth making a constant clicking like a hyperactive woodpecker.

Out of the claustrophobic paleness, Dr. Z rose up slowly, trudging ever nearer. The gorge opened next to me, invitingly. I looked over the ridge into a milky eternity of the canyon. A single step in the wrong direction—and you could be lost forever.

When I looked back, there was a second figure moving up behind Dr. Z. I stared at it and wiped a frozen fist across my face.

Out from a drifting snow bank, the figure seemed to float, reaching out a long arm for Dr. Z's back.

Tack, tack, tack.

I blinked and it was gone.

Dr. Z pointed the barrel of his pistol at my chattering face.

Then it was back—and it looked very familiar.

I squinted, coughed, and said, "Dad?"

Dr. Z swiveled to glance behind him.

Through the monochromatic scene, my father seemed to touch Z's eyes with icy fingers. The doctor leaned away and lost his footing. His mouth opened in a scream, but the swarming snow swallowed all sound. His arms went out. wind-milling. The gun disappeared in the air. His body tipped, dropping into the billowing vortex of whiteness below us.

He was gone.

And so was my dad. Instead, the figure now looked more like Slate Toriano, the Firewrangler.

CHAPTER 26

Through clicking incisors, I gasped out, "Hey, Ikimo," as he hovered over me, seeming to elevate me effortlessly and guide me back to the building's front entrance.

It was still night, but a night that glowed with a chilling creamy wind. The remains of the two bodies were still on the terrace and so was the bomb.

I had to go see if it was still ticking.

Another four inches of snow had built up, covering the device. When I wiped it away with my sleeve, I saw that the clock was still ticking and set for ten p.m.

Of course.

And it was nine-fifty-eight, of course. I laughed at the absolute absurdity of the situation.

"Cut the red wire," someone shouted.

I looked down and mumbled, "There are three red wires."

"Rewind the hands on the clock," came from a little nearer.

"No hands. Just buttons," I groaned,

"Reset the 'hour' button."

I felt faint from exhaustion. My vision blurred. "The button will only move forward, not back."

"Unplug it, stupid!" And a hand reached around me and pulled out the electric cord. I struggled to gaze up at my pal, Werewolf Weirick.

✧✧✧

He got me into the car and drove down the side of the mountain and out of the heaviest snow fall. The guard trucks were gone, God only knew where.

"Where's the doctor?" Norm asked, steering us over a spot of black ice.

Fighting the vestiges of snow-blindness, I said, "He fell into a deep depression."

"Sicko-psycho."

He had used the gun I'd given him to hijack one of the guard trucks. "They were all busy hustling the heck out of there. They must have known the bomb would be set to go off at ten o'clock."

"You could have been shot," I chattered. "Can you turn up the heat?"

He reached for the control knob next to the AM radio. "The bug transmitting from under your shirt helped me find you, but there was really only one place you could have been, what with your car parked near that building and all."

"I can't believe that you called me stupid."

"You shouldn't have left me behind, Mr. Wade."

"Glad I did. You still mad about it?"

"Sort of. I thought we were partners."

I chuckled at that and then winced from the real pain in my neck. "I've got one for you. Ready?"

He steered us to where the rest of our group waited at the dam. "Go for it."

"Oh, the monkeys have no tails in Zamboanga. The monkeys have no—"

"I know. They've been bitten off by whales. It's from *A Hole in the Head*."

I grinned and eased into a warm fuzzy slumber. Funny, I thought it was from Ford's *They Were Expendable*.

❧❧❧

I'd lost a lot of blood and woke a day later in a hospital room, startled to see an IV bottle dripping clear fluid down a long tube into my arm. "Get it out!"

"Hey, easy there, squirrel."

"It'll poison me. That stuff will kill me."

"Nah, it's good for ya. Hold still. Nurse! Need your help here, nurse!"

An elderly woman in white hustled in, adjusted the liquid flowing into my arm, and turned the lights out. In my head.

ↄ⁊ↄↄ

Then came the cops.

Due to the nitro explosion and the bodies of Rosita and the dead "Guy," I had to go through several Q and A meetings with the state highway patrol and reps from a couple of federal agencies. I regretted the death of Rosita, of course, but could not care less about the remains of Lombard. And that, as they say, was life.

I told my story over and over and, eventually, they went away and let me heal. I knew there was a summons or a subpoena headed my way, but I didn't mind. It came with the territory sometimes.

With Lex's help, I placed a call to Happy's Hacienda in Texas and settled up with Ford and Wayne. The actor/director had gotten off with only having to give written testimony, so the movie was still on track for completion, unless it rained again.

When I asked about Slate, I learned that the Firewrangler had almost died last night. He'd gotten up around eleven p.m. their time and somehow stumbled outside. When they found him, he was staring into nowhere and reaching his fingers into the night sky.

They said he was now relaxing and recovering, so I

promised I'd call back to speak with him and maybe even send some flowers.

Wayne laughed. "Yeah, he'll love that. Says he's thinking about getting into the confidential investigations industry."

Hey-bobba-rebop.

I had to keep my head tilted to one side due to the bandage taped to my neck so I sort of looked like the victim of a vampire. An inch more to my left and I'd have bled out in thirty seconds they said.

The hospital released me the next day into Suzi's care. She bundled me off to her apartment where I watched nothing but westerns on her living room TV. I didn't know that her couch was a hide-a-bed.

She had a remote control, so I clicked and watched the *Lone Ranger*, followed by the first of a series of *Swamp Fox* shows on Walt's program, followed by that new heart-throb, Clint Eastwood in *Rawhide* and finally the *Late Show Movie* with—what else?—Ford and Wayne's *Stagecoach*.

"Hollywood doesn't have smog," I told Suzi. "It has gunsmoke."

She brought me another Dixie cup of orange juice. "T'aint funny, Mr. Magoo."

In the morning, we drove to her office, listening to Paul Anka's "Lonely Boy" and the Everly Brother's "'Til I Kissed You" on the radio. There, in the sixth-floor conference room, I told my story all over again. Most of it the gang had already heard from Norm—as Brad was quick to point out.

Suzi surprised me by showing me an office that looked out at the Pantages theater across Hollywood Boulevard. They'd held the Academy Awards there earlier in the year. Looking down, I could see a cluster of people below in the street, protesting the tax assessment for the new "Walk of the Stars" program.

Hollywood, my home town. Land of fancy and fantasy, so much so its citizens needed a big white sign on a hill to remind them where they lived.

Suzi had been asked to be a consultant for a new TV show—something called *Honey West*. Brad was working on the Artie Shaw case now. Lex was thinking about buying a new wig, saying that she always wanted to be a redhead. Norm asked me to read the pages from his new screen play, and I almost gave him a Danny Thomas coffee spritz.

Around two o'clock in the afternoon, I went back to my crummy office at the Brown Derby, planning on packing up a few things. Sorting through my meager belongings, I found a phone message from the day before. Some movie director over at Fox that I'd never heard of, Alan Smithee, wanted to hire me to find a "lost" film.

I sat down in the swivel chair behind my desk and carefully peeled away some of the bandage from my neck. I opened a desk drawer and took out my own magic eight-ball.

Shaking and turning it over, I read: *OUTLOOK GOOD*.

Maybe I'd keep the office here open just a little longer. Until the end of the year—or until the wedding.

THE END

The Facts Behind the Fiction

John Wayne ~ Perhaps America's most famous actor, who nearly went bankrupt from producing and directing *The Alamo*.

John Ford ~ Perhaps America's most famous director, whose social consciousness evolved while at the recreated Alamo.

Philip K. Dick ~ Perhaps America's most famous science fiction writer.

Mount Baldy ~ The last place you would look for a mass killer.

Paramount ~ Stan's favorite studio, perhaps because nobody ever shot at him there—yet.

Joe Canutt ~ Son of the legendary Yakima and said to have almost died making *Ben-Hur* and other gags.

Alan Smithee ~ Perhaps the most famous director who never existed.

LSD ~ D-lysergic acid, silent snow, secret snow.

The Taft ~ Big brown blocky building at Hollywood and Vine.

Yurba Buena ~ Island near a treasure in the bay.

Allen Ginsberg ~ Perhaps the most howling beat-generation poet.

Jerry Lewis ~ Perhaps the most original movie mad man of the latter half of the twentieth century.

Charles M. Smith ~ Got thirty years in prison.

John "Bert" Adams ~ Phillies catcher with low RBI, RIP.

Time magazine ~ October, 1959, issue signals the end of TV's cowboys and the start of private eyes, and later spies.

Sutro's ~ San Franciscans used to line up here for baths.

Panhandle Park ~ Where Haight met Ashbury.

Lefty O'Doul ~ Seal's coach and restaurateur.

Miles Archer ~ SF investigator who met Orson and later Martians.

If you enjoyed

STORMFALL

Turn the page for a preview of

STANFALL

The next book in the

Stan Wade, LA PI series

Coming soon from
John Hegenberger
and Black Opal Books

CHAPTER 1

January, 1960:

I was uncomfortable that day in early January for a lot of reasons.

I didn't like the chair Suzi had provided in my new office at Sunset Investigations. It was too high for the glass-topped desk, and I couldn't figure out how to get it down so my knees didn't bang into the drawer where I kept my new business cards and my old gun.

I didn't like the view out the office's side window either. I could see down Hollywood Boulevard from up here on the sixth floor of the Taft, but between the haze of smog and the crush of other brick and concrete buildings as far as Grauman's Chinese, the whole perspective was pure urban clutter.

I much more preferred to sit on the fantail of my boat

and watch the surf roll in from the Pacific to crash into the Santa Monica pier.

I also didn't like the formality of working in a structured office environment, even if my best girl was in charge and few of my close friends were here learning how to operate as private investigators. It felt like I was mixing business with pleasure, and my personal life had been taken over by my professional life. *I'm becoming one of those Organization Men.*

I recalled my little office at the rear of the Brown Derby on Wilshire and found myself yearning. It had been noisy and smelly back there beside the restaurant's steaming kitchen, but it had been home.

What now made me the most uncomfortable, however, was the thought that a presidential candidate had called the agency, asking for help with a confidential matter—but he didn't want yours truly on the case. Instead, Kennedy's aide said that the campaign wanted to hire the girl of my dreams and new boss, Suzi.

Somehow, that made me feel a whole lot older than twenty-nine. I'd worked for almost a decade building up a reputation in this biz, first as an apprentice eye for Mr. P and then with my own agency, all before joining Sunset. The idea of playing second fiddle to a woman, albeit the woman I was going to marry in a few months, set my nerves on edge and made me tap the tip of a sharpened pencil on the glass desktop.

1959 had been a hell of a year for me. Maybe I needed a vacation. Fishing up in Tahoe sounded mighty appealing. So did a cruise down to Mexico. So did two fingers of Bushmills.

I shook my head. "This is looney tunes."

And as if it had heard me and wanted to strike up a conversation, my shiny desk phone buzzed. Not rang, like any decent telephone. The black instrument, with its integral speaker and flashing red light, buzzed at me like an angry wasp.

I almost swatted it. Pushing the amber button, I croaked, "What?"

"Man here to see you." Weezie's voice sounded tiny and tinny. "Says his name is Dick Van Dyke, if you can believe it. He wants to hire you."

I was delighted in the prospect. So much so that I affected my best Bogart lisp. "Shoo him in, sweetheart. Shoo him in."

I adjusted my butt in the chair, starting to feel comfortable.

About the Author

John Hegenberger writes adventure, mystery, science, and horror fiction. Born and raised in the heart of the heartland, Columbus, Ohio, he is the author of *Tripleye* series and the *Stan Wade LA PI* series from Black Opal Books. Father of three, a tennis enthusiast, collector of silent films and OTR, hiker, Francophile, B.A. Comparative Literature, ex-navy, ex-comic book dealer, ex-marketing exec at Exxon, AT&T, and IBM, he has been happily married for forty-seven years.

Over the years, he's published two non-fiction books about collecting pop-culture movie memorabilia and comic books and sold half a dozen stories to magazines and anthologies. Follow his adventures at johnhegenberger.com and have fun.

9 781626 946057